THE LEGEND OF TARO TSUJIMOTO

THE UNAUTHORIZED, FICTIONAL BIOGRAPHY

Mark Hinrich

Copyright © 2016 Mark Hinrich
Printed in the United States of America

THE LEGEND OF TARO TSUJIMOTO: The Unauthorized, Fictional Biography/ Hinrich- 1st Edition

ISBN: 978-0-9978317-3-3

1. Hockey. 2. National Hockey League. 3. Fiction. 4. Sports.
5. Faux Biography 6. Hinrich.

This is a work of fiction. All characters in this novel are fictitious. Any resemblance to actual events or locations, unless specified, or persons, living or dead is entirely coincidental.

No part of this book may be reproduced or transmitted in any form by any means, electronic or mechanical, including photocopying, recording, or by any information storage and retrieval system without permission in writing by the
author.

NFB
<<<>>>
No Frills Buffalo/Amelia Press
119 Dorchester Road
Buffalo, New York 14213

For more information visit

nofrillsbuffalo.com

For Mary Lou and Sally, who encouraged me even when I didn't know it.

THE LEGEND OF TARO TSUJIMOTO

Preface

You may not have heard of him... Then again, who has?

He was drafted in 1974, 183rd overall, by Buffalo, but never made it to the NHL.

Then again, he never had a chance.

It wasn't because of a lack of talent. No, what prevented Taro Tsujimoto from breaking into the league was simply the fact that he never existed.

Up until 1980, the event was a closed affair for the general public with only General Managers and League officials allowed to be present. Teams would either meet at designated hotel conference rooms, or the NHL would conduct the draft via conference call as was the case in 1974.

At that time, with only 18 franchises in the League, the draft was permitted to extend beyond nine rounds (it was eventually reduced to seven rounds in 2005) if teams continued to select players.

As the 11th round came around, Buffalo had finally had enough.

The Legend of Taro Tsujimoto

Bored and exhausted with the tedium of looking at players that had a slim chance of ever making the roster, Buffalo's General Manager decided to pull one of the more creative pranks in team history, let alone in NHL history.

The scouting director perked up. "Wouldn't it be great if someone would take a player who isn't eligible for the draft?"

He enlisted the public relations director to create a fictional player.

Sending a secretary to find some common Japanese names, they soon came up with the imaginary Taro Tsujimoto of the Tokyo Katanas - literally translating to the Tokyo Sabres (Katana is a type of Japanese samurai sword).

When the League President asked Buffalo for their selection, he was met with laughter from around the League. International scouting wasn't as prevalent as it is in the NHL now, and drafting a player from Japan wasn't exactly a common practice. The JIHL, Japanese International Hockey League, although it was a real entity, had no team representing Tokyo at that time.

Buffalo's GM carefully spelled the name of his invented centerman, which was printed in every record book and media guide in the League. It was also reported by major media outlets including *The Hockey News*.

When the bewildered league president asked for clarification, received it, then spelled back "Taro Tsujimo-

to" letter by letter, the four men holed up in the directors room at Memorial Auditorium in Buffalo struggled to suppress their laughter. "It's not like it was Brown or Jones or something. It just slowed the draft down even more." The proceedings mercifully ended after the selection of 247 players.

All but one of them was real.

Keep in mind that the NHL at that time was only beginning to expand its reach for players. Scandinavian players were beginning to be drafted and play in the NHL around that time. Although players from the Soviet Union, an international powerhouse at the time, were off-limits, it would not have been out of line for a team to be scouting for new talent in unusual places, which is why no one made a huge fuss over this selection.

Reporters in the following weeks grilled team reps about the arrival of Tsujimoto to Buffalo. The response was simple; the prospect would come soon.

Of course, he never did and finally the team gave in and confessed to the gag prior to the start of training camp. But to this day there are some publications that list the 183rd overall selection from Tokyo.

And the myth lives on...

...and that's where our story begins...

Introduction

It was incredibly difficult, nearly impossible to track down accurate information on Taro Tsujimoto. Many records were never transferred to any form of electronic media, and therefore are lost to history.

After Taro made it to the NHL, some effort was made to try and piece his back-story together. With the help of his father, Hiro, some information was pieced together about Taro's playing days.

Taro himself was not initially interested in being interviewed for this tale. He maintained that he was just another player in the NHL, and would ask why it was worth the effort to tell his story when many other players had stories of their own to be told? There were bigger stars in hockey that should have their tales told by someone.

However, after much effort on the part of Buffalo , with whom he spent the bulk of his career, Taro started to come around. He finally agreed to share his magical tale with the world. His wife, Taylor, would help bring him around.

Chapter 1

Who would have thought that a hockey player from Japan would be so popular in the NHL? Well, let me tell you about a certain young man who went from completely unknown to hero in the eyes of North American hockey.

His name is Taro Tsujimoto. He first rose to fame in the Japanese International Hockey League, a little known league in the country of Japan. That league got started with Canadians who were still in the country after World War Two. The sport took off, and soon interest had spread to the kids.

Taro was born on November 16th, 1954, in Osaka, Japan. Not much is known about his parents, other than his father, Hiro, was apparently instrumental in founding the Japanese Hockey League. He was also a powerful force in creating a junior league for kids to get regular playing time.

Young Taro took a liking to ice skating and the game of hockey at an early age, and Hiro helped nurture and direct his son's interest. We don't know much else about young Taro, though. Records and information are sketchy from that time.

As Taro entered his teenage years, he had become quite the center, quickly developing an on-ice vision seen by few of his time, let alone later on in the professional leagues.

Taro was a big fan of Montreal, and who would have disagreed with that choice of teams? Montreal was extremely successful throughout the nineteen-sixties and seventies in the NHL. No doubt, he followed Montreal fairly closely, as close as possible for that time. He had plenty of heroes in the NHL, and it is fairly certain that he tried his best to emulate them.

There is little to suggest that when the NHL expanded in 1967 that Taro thought of playing in the NHL. After all, he was playing hockey in an obscure corner of the world. He almost certainly would not have paid much attention when Vancouver and Buffalo entered the NHL in 1970. It's nearly guaranteed that he wouldn't have ever thought of playing in Buffalo. His dream, which he confided at the time of this writing, was to play for Montreal. Failing that, he figured he would go play for Toronto and wear their historic blue and white.

Of course, fate had a different idea for young Taro. As it turned out, he would get to play in both Montreal and Toronto, against his favorite teams.

Draft Year

As the 1974 NHL Draft approached, Taro was having a banner year. He scored a career high fifteen goals and twenty-five points. It should be remembered, though, that his league in Tokyo only played a much shorter season. So those numbers should be kept in context.

On the other hand, Taro's team, the Katanas, did not fare so well in the league that year, finishing out of the playoffs near the bottom of the Northern Conference. It was a crushing blow to a young hockey player with big dreams. He still dreamed of making the top league in Japan, and even wanted to play for his home-town team in Osaka.

Life was about to offer him a new opportunity, however.

Someone in the NHL passed along Taro's name as "undiscovered talent." No one knew anything about Japanese hockey players. It was barely known that there was even a hockey system in that country.

As far as Taro was concerned, he might be draft-eligible, but he had about the longest route to the league that anyone could possibly have. Taro had explored options in North America, and had even talked to a junior hockey team in the city of New Westminster, located just outside Vancouver, British Columbia. The Western Canadian Hockey League was a key developmental league in Canada. It was considered one of the best routes to pro hockey. New Westminster was interested in bringing him in to training camp as a non-roster invitee. Basically, they were going to give him an invitation, and see what skills he had. If he impressed enough, then he might even crack the roster. He would be an eighteen- year-old rookie, and that would no doubt put him in a difficult position. But it was at least something to consider. Taro preferred to think about his options with a club in the minor leagues instead, on the theory that the minors would offer a better chance of making it to the top of the heap, the NHL.

Young Taro began to consider North American hockey more seriously, and that's when the fateful phone call came, and changed his life forever.

The Buffalo Sabres called him the day after the 1974 NHL Entry Draft, with surprising news. Taro Tsujimoto, of the Tokyo Katanas, had been drafted with the 183rd pick in the 11th round. No doubt, his father, Hiro, was ecstatic. Taro would have the opportunity to become the first Japanese player ever to make it to the NHL. Just being drafted gave him the status of first to do so.

Now the tough part would begin... and this is where our tale gets really interesting.

Anyone could get drafted, it seemed. With a couple hundred picks in the 1974 NHL Draft, players were selected from all over Canada, and a few from the United States as well.

In addition to the NHL, there was also the World Hockey Association. The WHA was considered a rival league; much of the NHL refused to even acknowledge their existence. However, by the 1974-75 season, it was becoming clear that the WHA was a force to be reckoned with, and NHL teams were losing players to the WHA left and right. Not only that, but the WHA was willing to look to Europe and non-traditional hockey markets in order to look for more talent. This would bode well for Taro as he approached training camp with the Sabres. It certainly opened up the possibilities of playing professional hockey in North America. If the NHL didn't work out, he might have a chance to catch on with a club in the WHA. Rumor had it that the Houston Aeros were interested in signing Taro if he didn't want or was unable to agree to terms with Buffalo.

The mere idea of a Japanese player in the NHL was a novelty to many around the league. For weeks over the summer, no one took the idea seriously. Upper management with many teams didn't even think that Taro was a real player, instead choosing to believe that he was a fake name thrown in as a joke.

Taro would have to work extra hard to shed any labels. No doubt, he hoped to earn a roster spot on his own merits, but still questions abounded about his abilities. Could he stand up to a full season in the NHL? More importantly, would he be able to stand up physically to the bigger players during the season, let alone a single game? Taro stood just five foot eight inches tall, and weighed in at 165 pounds. Sure, he may have been big by Japanese hockey standards, but in the NHL, a player of that size would have to be extremely fast to avoid getting pounded into the boards in a game.

Still, he was going to rookie camp with the Sabres, and they would at least give him a chance. That's what he wanted most; a chance to prove himself. The rest would, no doubt, sort itself out in time. Whether he made it or not, he would already make history as the first Japanese hockey player to go to NHL training camp.

But Taro wanted more, much more. He wanted to be on the Sabres opening night roster, and play in the league on a regular basis. It would be an interesting time at rookie camp. The Sabres top two draft picks no doubt would receive much of the hype. Both were excellent draft picks. Taro wanted to be with them on opening night. He thought very highly of his skills and confidence.

So, Taro spent a lot of time at the ice rink over that summer. He worked with many Japanese hockey players in Tokyo. He showed a lot of speed, and a keen eye around the net. He could thread a pass through seemingly impossible spaces. But there was no real method of simulating the constant pounding that he would suffer from players much taller and stronger than himself.

Unfortunately, he had some doubts as he boarded the first of several airplanes on his way to Buffalo's training camp. The most important doubt in his mind? How well could even the best Japanese hockey player, let alone someone of his above-average talent, make it to the NHL? There was just no way to know until he reached camp and demonstrated his skills.

Taro was filled with doubt as he prepared to leave Tokyo. His father was guardedly optimistic about the prospects of Taro actually being able to make it in the North American game. The biggest worry was the extremely physical nature of the game. During the 1970s, the NHL was full of line brawls and some of the toughest players to ever play the game. Taro was going to eventually face teams like Philadelphia, also known as the "Broad Street Bullies," who were making a near-mockery of the game with their goon tactics. The Flyers roster featured players with childish names like "Big Bird," "Hammer" and "Hound Dog."

Taro was barely five foot eight inches tall. He had succeeded in Japan because he was taller than much of his league opponents. Now, he was going to face players that were several inches taller, and a lot meaner than he was, and would be expected to survive on the ice on a nightly basis. It was going to be his biggest challenge ever. Would Taro be able to use his superior speed and fly up and down the ice, or would he become a novelty, the first Japanese player to make it to the NHL, but only play a couple of games before being forced out? Only time would tell, but Taro was supremely confident. He felt he was faster than anyone else in North America. He would be able to race up and down the ice, avoiding the big hits that cause injuries. He insisted that his game would adapt well to the NHL. His father finally decided that Taro was going to do this whether or not he gave approval, so Hiro and Taro came to an agreement that Taro would fly to Buffalo and make his attempt at the NHL.

There was a lot of optimism at home the night before Taro headed east. He recalls the following from that night:

> "I was nervous. This would be the first time I would be away from family for more than a few days at a time. Would it bother me? Sure, but I had to take advantage of this opportunity. I would never know if I could make it in the NHL if I never went to Buffalo. They had used a late round draft pick on me, and I wanted to prove that I was worth so much more than that late pick. My father wanted me to go, but my mother wasn't so sure that being gone that long would be good for me. She finally agreed that I should pursue this opportunity, a chance to make it at the highest level of hockey. My father said that I carried the honor of Japanese hockey with me, and I should hold my head

up high and be proud of everything that I was representing, and be the very best that I could be. I promised to be honorable, uphold the family name, and the honor of the entire country of Japan."

So, the fateful day had arrived. Taro, along with his father, departed Tokyo and headed toward the United States, and a date with history. The long trip gave the youngster a lot of time to think and reflect on what was to come. They somehow managed to make it all the way without losing any luggage, always a concern of air travelers, much more so for a young hockey player trying to haul his gear around the world.

Taro arrived in town just two days before camp was to begin. The night before he was to report to camp, Taro was undoubtedly nervous. It is rumored that he was beginning to have second thoughts after he realized how much different this new country, with a new language and new way of life was going to be. Fortunately, for history's sake, his father was able to keep him on track.

Who knows what would have become of Taro had he not stayed just twelve hours longer?

That was a question, fortunately, that would not need to be asked.

Chapter 2
Training Camp

That fateful day that Taro had both dreaded and looked forward to had finally arrived. It was time for training camp to begin. His father, Hiro, drove him to the arena and left him there for the day, with a promise to pick him up and return to the hotel in the evening.

Young Taro would spend much of that first day going through a lot of medical check-ups. This was rookie camp, and would consist of drafted players, plus other non-roster invites. Basically, there would be a lot of first timers. Out of this large group, only the very best and talented, with the most promise, would advance to main camp with the returning roster of Buffalo players. Taro knew that he would have to prove himself early when it was time to start skating. Fortunately, he was supremely confident in his conditioning, having spent a lot of time back in Tokyo running up and down stairs and riding his bicycle around town for hours on end. In addition, the diet of the typical Japanese consisted of a lot of fish, very healthy for Taro. He felt this might give him an edge over the North American diet.

As it turned out, Taro was in excellent shape. He would end up finishing in the top three percent of all rookies in overall conditioning, although he was somewhat lower in weight lifting. Sure, the Canadian players were able to lift more weight, but Taro believed that his speed, vision and play-making abilities would compensate for the lack of bulk on his five foot eight inch frame.

This would prove to be a prophetic belief.

The first day of skating drills was the chance Taro had been waiting for, and he showed off at the very first opportunity. The initial end to end rush showed off his straight line skating, while the obstacle course gave him a chance to shine even further. One of the veteran players in training camp recalls:

> **"Taro had unbelievable speed from day one. I knew that I was a fairly fast player myself, but this young Japanese kid looked like he could skate circles around me, and not even work hard. I made it my business right away to get to know him a little better. Maybe, working together, we could both make the team and help each other."**

As rookie camp progressed, no doubt the team officials

watching from above were forced to take notice of Taro. He was making rookie goalies look silly with his abilities. Taro's shot wasn't the fastest or hardest, but it did seem to be more accurate than most players in camp. He had an uncanny knack for hitting corners or the infamous five-hole, the space between the goalie's skates.

But it was his play-making and passing ability that almost scared some goalies. Taro could thread a pass through the most impossible of spaces to a teammate. He would show this skill off time and time again during the course of rookie camp. Often, Buffalo's top draft picks would be a more than willing recipient of these passes, and he would bury the shots as the goalie scrambled across the net to try and block the shot.

Both Taro and these top picks would go on to main camp, along with a couple others as well. They were ecstatic, but knew that the hard work had just begun.

Taro remembers sitting in the hotel with his father the night before main camp began.

"I was very pleased to be going to main camp with the Sabres. This was a very great honor, and I believed that the Japanese hockey players would be very pleased with my progress. Still, I had a lot to accomplish. I was not satisfied with just making it to training camp.

I wanted to play in the pre-season games, and then I wanted to make it to the opening night roster. I wanted a career in the NHL, not just a game or two. I was determined to make it and would not quit."

Main camp started out with the requisite medical check-ups for everyone, even the rookies joining camp. Again, Taro excelled, finishing near the very top of all players in camp. Many of the veteran players were very impressed with the play of young Taro, and he would play alongside all of them at times in camp, to see how he performed. Martin, in particular, asked the coaches if he could play wing to Taro's center position, to see what the young Japanese player could do. Buffalo's famed "French Connection" thought quite highly of Taro already, and two of the three showed great interest playing with Taro as well. They even hinted to other players that Taro might be able to join the team straight away, as an eighteen-year-old rookie.

When the pre-season schedule began, Taro was assigned to two games as the number two center on the team. Taro performed far better than expectations. Of course, as a late round pick, expectations were understandably low.

To be realistic, Taro didn't have anything to lose by attending camp and staying into the pre-season. No one expected him to attend camp, and there was almost no chance before camp started that he would have stayed at all. The fact that Taro would even be playing in a pre-season game surprised experts all over the NHL. Sabres management began to think that a star was being born, a star from the land of the Rising Sun. This forced the team to negotiate a contract with Taro. He would sign a three-year entry level deal, of which the terms of the deal would not be discussed outside of the office. With the deal in place, Taro was free to play in the pre-season for Buffalo.

When Taro helped set up three goals at home against Boston in his first pre-season game, the fans were instantly won over. His teammates were likely won over as well. Taro showed a chemistry with one player in particular, a high draft pick named Danny, the type of synergy that seemed to indicate the two had been playing for years, and not mere days. Another player, a long-time vet, spent a lot of time playing left wing with Danny and Taro, and also helped keep the other team's players from roughing up Taro as well. The "muscleman" was an excellent deterrent for opposition players who had eyes on slowing down the speedy Taro. One of the veteran Buffalo players took Taro aside just before that first game in Boston. He recalls:

"I told Taro, plain and simple, he was going to get hit. He would get hit hard, and often. That was the nature of the NHL. He was going to have to let me and

other teammates help him, or he was going to be left to his own devices. To be honest, I knew the kid wouldn't make it two days without backup. He understood right away, though. He shook my hand, then took two steps back and bowed very deeply toward me. He explained that he was showing me deep respect with that gesture. I returned that bow, matching the respect. I think those few minutes cemented a bond between him and I. At that moment, I knew the kid was going to go places, because he had the sense to listen to a veteran player. You don't often see that in a rookie, especially someone who was drafted so late. Taro really had his priorities in order."

Whether for good or worse, Taro was held out of the pre-season game against Philadelphia. The thinking was most likely that Taro wasn't ready to be pushed around by the Broad Street Bullies. No doubt, Taro was thankful to be watching that game.

Taro recalls the following from that night:

"Those Philadelphia players were rough to the point of being dangerous. I was happy not to be on the ice for that hockey game."

By the end of the pre-season schedule, Buffalo's management had some tough decisions to make. First and foremost was the fate of Taro Tsujimoto. Would he stay on the Sabres roster, or would he go to the minor league, and play for Hershey. Another option was to send him to a junior league for a season and let him get used to the North American game at a lower level, against people his own age.

It was probably the suggestions of several of the players that tipped the scales. They asked specifically if Taro was going to be there with them. They campaigned for the youngster to make the opening night roster, based on the chemistry between the three players. The head coach enthusiastically agreed, and history was to be made on October 10th, 1974.

Taro had a couple of days to mull this over before opening night. His father, Hiro, was to return to Japan on October 12th. He would only see his son's first game of the season, then fly back home. Taro would stay in a motel near the arena for the first few games, while his fate was determined.

Oh, one more little detail had to be decided; his jersey number. Most rookies get high numbers. This is because the established veterans get to use their regular numbers in camp and pre-season. However, once the opening night roster is determined, usually players will select or be given a lower number. It was unusual to see numbers above forty. With no hesitation at all, Taro selected number 74. He stated, firmly, that this represented his draft year. After a little discussion, the team gave in and allowed the unusually high number. Few players at that time wore such high numbers. Who would have known at the time that 74 would become such a popular number? Who, indeed.

...and so, we arrive at opening night.

Opening Night

Prior to the game, a tribute to a former Sabres captain and NHL All-Star was held. The memorial marked the untimely death of the well-known and well-liked player who had died in an automobile accident on February 21st, 1974. It was a solemn proceeding. Taro watched quietly as the hockey arena went silent for a full minute.

With that concluded, the team proceeded to the opening ceremonies. All the players were introduced, including one Taro Tsujimoto, becoming the first Japanese player to play in the NHL regular season.

Taro would, in fact, make a quick impact in his very first game. With on-ice vision that would become legendary, he would thread a pass through two Boston players to Danny, who would bury the pass for a goal just 18 seconds into the first game of the season. While Danny would keep that puck, the coaching staff would ask Taro to sign a puck, in Japanese, after that first game. This historic puck would be displayed in the front of the Buffalo Memorial Auditorium, where the Sabres played their home games.

Taro would get his first career goal two games later. That puck went straight to Taro, and he took it home. The Hockey Hall of Fame came calling, and asked for it. Knowing what it meant to the young Japanese player, the Sabres arranged for a different puck, signed by Taro, to make its way to the Hall of Fame, along with the jersey from opening night. Now, with a career of just three NHL games, Taro could rightfully boast that he was already in the Hall of Fame.

Taro wouldn't score a lot of goals that first season, but he quickly became a fan favorite for his speed and passing ability. It was in early to mid-December that fans started posting signs for Taro around the arena.

The soon-to-be infamous "Taro says..." signs would often comment on either Taro himself, Buffalo, or sometimes take a humorous dig at the other team. T-shirts and buttons would soon be available with the moniker "Taro says..." at the team store. While not the best player on the team, Taro was quickly gaining a cult-like following in Buffalo. Taro himself thought they were a lot of fun, even if sometimes he didn't get the joke. He recalls:

> "The signs and shirts with my name were a lot of fun for the fans. I didn't always understand the joke people were making, but I thought, as long as it is in good taste, it can't be a bad thing. A rookie like myself can always use positive press to help promote himself to the league. Sabres management seemed to like it as well. When the signs started appearing in other build-

ings, on the road, I knew that I was becoming a star in the league. At some point during that first season, I showed the team how to spell out my first name in Japanese, and soon the signs, in Japanese, began to show up in the arena as well. The fans were really getting behind me from my first games. One of my teammates told me that it was like a fan club. Then my teammate had to explain what a fan club was."

By the end of December, in spite of a two-game losing streak to end the year, the Sabres had a very impressive 24 win, 8 loss, and 5 tie record, one of the best in the league. However, things were about to get even better. After a January 9th loss to Los Angeles, the team would lose just two more games by the end of February, a period of twenty-three games. Buffalo would clinch a spot in the playoffs on February 16th, and would clinch the division title with a win over California on March 23rd. It would take a win in the final game of the season, however, to finally clinch the conference title.

For Taro, it was a magical mystery tour, of sorts. He would play in all 80 games, scoring a total of 21 goals, with 29 assists, for an overall total of 50 points. It was well beyond anything the young Japanese player would have ever expected. While Taro would not win rookie of the year honors, he would, however, earn a nod to the all-rookie, second team. His teammate, and friend Danny would have an excellent rookie season as well, scoring 31 goals and 62 overall points. The two had shown considerable chemistry in their first season, and it would continue into the playoffs.

Oh, yes, Taro had made the playoffs in his first year. But, the wonderful ride for Buffalo wasn't even close to finishing yet.

Taro became good friends with fellow rookie Danny. While Taro was having some trouble adjusting to the North American game, Danny was having a much easier time. He would finish his rookie year with 62 points in 78 games. He recalls:

> "Philadelphia won the Cup the year before, and they were a very physical team. Somewhat intimidating as well. I can't recall winning a game in Philly during the Finals, but we took them to six games. The real key to their victory was their goalie, Bernie. He was a huge star in goal, and I'm certain that he made a huge difference."

1974-75 Playoffs

Buffalo, by virtue of their superior record, had a first round bye, and would meet Chicago in the Quarter-Finals. It would be a hard-fought five game series, with Taro's team emerging victorious. Taro would finish that series with two assists, both setting up key goals in the series. He wasn't worried about not getting goals yet. He knew that his inexperience would be a factor in a lack of ice time, and that was true for this series. However, it was also true that when Taro was on the ice, he was quickly gaining needed experience. He wouldn't be slowed down as the playoffs progressed.

Montreal was the next opponent. This was the team Taro had idolized growing up. It was also the team that Taro had dreamed of being part of, should he make it to the NHL. While fate sent him elsewhere in the NHL, it was fitting that the conference should be contested against Taro's dream team.

In Game 1, Taro again showed his flair for the dramatic, threading a pass up the middle of the ice rink to Danny, who would bury the overtime, game winning goal. In Game 2, Taro again helped decide the game, with key assists to lead the way to a 4-2 win.

Montreal would take the next two games at home by a combined 15-2 score. Taro was demoralized, watching his childhood heroes destroy his current club.

Returning home for Game 5, however, Buffalo fell behind 3-1 early, but eventually would claim victory in overtime, and when Taro set up two goals in the first period of Game 6, the Sabres would be able to withstand a Montreal rally in the third period and win the series.

Taro had proven himself worthy of his roster spot, notching four assists in the Montreal series. A teammate recalls:

> "It was quite impressive watching Taro in the Montreal series. I think that was where he finally came into his own, emerging as a star on the team. Remember, this kid was barely nineteen, and living in a foreign country, with a foreign language to deal with as well. The fact that he overcame those obstacles and managed to do everything he did in the season and playoffs, well, I take my hat off to him."

Unfortunately, Philadelphia would prove to be more difficult than Montreal. The Flyers would score four goals to win Game 1. they would also hold Buffalo without a single shot on goal for much of the third period in Game 2, taking a 2-0 series lead back to Buffalo.

Still, optimism was high returning home. No one expected, however, the heavy fog in the arena. The game was stopped 12 times because of the fog. Even stranger, one of the Buffalo players spotted a bat flying around the arena. He swung his stick and killed it. Unfortunately, many superstitious Buffalo fans came to look at that event as an evil omen.

Buffalo would recover from a three-goal deficit on a pair of goals 17 seconds apart. Yes, you guessed correctly; Taro set up both goals with slick passing. The overtime winning goal was scored in heavy fog, with the Flyers goalie unable to see the puck until it was too late.

Sadly, that would be the last game that Buffalo would win that playoff season. Philadelphia would take Game 5 at home, and then hang a shut out in Buffalo in Game 6 for the series-clinching win, earning the Stanley Cup.

After their success during the season, and through most of the playoffs, losing in the Finals proved to be a bitter pill to swallow. For Taro, personally, it was the end of his rookie season. He was ecstatic about the regular season, and most of the playoff run as well. Of course, he was disappointed about the end result. But he accepted defeat dogmatically. He recalls:

> "Of course, everyone wants to win the title, and be the very best. But only one team can claim that honor. I feel that Philadelphia earned that series win. Their

goalie deserved to win the MVP as well. I have learned so much from my teammates this season, and am confident that I will succeed in the future as well."

It's hard to believe that Taro was barely nineteen when he made that statement. He seemed much more mature than a lot of people gave him credit for. It definitely was a good sign for the youngster. His father, Hiro, was able to attend Games 3 and 4 in Buffalo, and was no doubt pleased with Taro's progress.

As the off-season began, changes in the roster would, of course, take place. Players would come and go. Some retired, some were traded. Some headed off to the WHA with the promise of a bigger contract. It was a crazy time for professional hockey, and Taro watched it all happen.

It had been a wild ride for his rookie season. Things were to change as the following season approached.

Chapter 3

Taro's second season would prove to be, statistically, a lot like his first. He would score 20 goals, and notch a total of 46 points. Both these totals were just slightly below his rookie numbers, however, the team was pleased with his overall progress.

The team itself, however, would only finish second in their division, and third overall in the conference. Overall, goal production was down somewhat, which contributed to their drop in the overall standings. On the upside, Taro had continued his chemistry with Danny, who would go on to score 50 goals that season, with many being set up by Taro.

His third season, the 1976-77 season, proved to be Taro's best to that point. He would score an impressive 30 goals for the first time, and finish with a total of 68 points. He was finally beginning to get the recognition that he so richly deserved. He proved durable as well, not missing a single game for the third consecutive season. But it was not without adventure.

One day, one event in particular, stands out from that season. It was the morning of January 28th, 1977, a Friday. Buffalo was scheduled to leave for Montreal late in the day, with a practice in the morning. Taro was preparing to leave for practice. A chance phone call from his father delayed him about fifteen minutes. That proved to be a costly delay.

He would never make it to the arena. It took him eight hours to make ultimately make it to the airport in time to meet the team for their trip to Montreal.

The winds were blowing at 29 miles an hour, gusting to 49. By high noon, the temperature had plummeted 26 degrees, crashing below zero. The wind was gusting so hard, almost 70 mph, that the wind chills were down between minus 60 and minus 70 degrees.

Thousands were stranded in offices, schools and factories as roads became impassable when as much as eight inches of snow fell or was blown off the frozen Lake Erie, on top of the 33 inches that had already choked Buffalo that winter. An estimated 13,000 people were stranded in downtown Buffalo alone, along with an estimated 8,000 cars clogging the roads of the city, many of which ended up completely buried. Some Sabres employees were forced to sleep overnight in the Sabres home rink "The Aud," among the 300 people who took shelter there.

High winds combined with the already unusual weather

conditions from that winter, leaving Lake Erie covered with ice. To make matters worse, a layer of snow on top of the ice was easily picked up by the winds and dumped on the Buffalo shores. Normally, the snow on the lake would go through a thaw-freeze cycle that would leave a hard crust on the top, and hold the snow down, keeping it from blowing into the city.

 Taro heard about several of his teammates and their problems over the next week. Yes, it took that long for the team to account for everyone.

 Buffalo's head coach was able to get to the airport, but only by following snow plows, and the 20-minute drive stretched it into two hours. Another player set out with his four-wheel-drive truck, dug out a teammate and headed off for the airport with three additional players along for the ride.

 By 3pm, Taro and a few other players had arrived at the airport, but not enough to fill out a roster for the game in Montreal. While Coach Smith was about to call ahead and cancel the game, yet another poor soul, who had managed to his four-wheel-drive vehicle only by jumping out of a window and shoveling his way to his garage, arrived with four other players, giving Buffalo enough bodies to make the trip.

 In spite of the stormy weather, the plane managed to leave Buffalo, and the team reached Montreal for the game that night. It was quite a flight, with a very bumpy ride most of the way to Montreal, at least until they managed to break out of the back end of the storm. However, Buffalo's play-by-play announcer was unable to make the flight to Montreal and was forced to call the game over the phone from his apartment while watching the game on television. Taro recalls:

> "I had never seen anything like this in my entire life. That was definitely the worst weather I have ever seen, and the most snow as well. I don't know how my teammates were able to make it to the airport, but we somehow managed to get enough people to the airport. We all traded stories for days about our experiences.
>
> I managed to get a ride with Danny to the airport. Fortunately, he knew how to drive in a mess like this. It still took almost an hour to get to the airport."

The Sabres rallied to limit Montreal to just five shots for the third period, to earn the plucky and shorthanded Buffalo squad an unexpected, if not unbelievable, 3-3 tie against the defending (and eventual) champions, outshooting them by a final margin of 27-19. It was a great way to cap off an unbelievable night.

However, the blizzard forced them to cancel the following night's game in Buffalo against the Los Angeles, a day when the winds continued to howl with gusts up to 52 mph. Monday, Taro and company boarded a bus for a 10-hour trip across New York State for a game against New York to start a three game road trip as the storm raged in Buffalo until Tuesday. Their next home game, against Toronto, was postponed, while everyone in the area recovered from the extreme weather. This meant that Buffalo went two weeks without a single home game. Taro recalls:

"I remember that we went a very long time between home games. It was terrible to watch all the devastation. I heard, later on, that there were 29 deaths related to the storm in western New York. Eleven of those unfortunate souls were in the City of Buffalo, and nine of them were buried in their cars. When we finally had another home game, there was a very long, sad minute of silence to remember those that had been lost in the great storm. It is definitely something that I will not forget for a very long time."

While the regular season held a lot of promise, finishing just two points out of the division title, Buffalo would not have a lot of playoff success. They would lose to New York in the quarter-finals in a four-game sweep. Taro himself was held to just one assist in the entire playoff run, leaving him terribly disappointed and frustrated.

Now, with three seasons under his belt, Taro was ready to negotiate a new contract with Buffalo. He felt that the team had treated him more than fairly, and opted to go into the negotiations himself. He knew what he wanted, and was prepared to ask for it.

When the two sides met, Taro was surprised to see that the Sabres were willing to offer much more than he was asking, and he accepted a three-year extension. The total time in the office discussing the deal was less than two hours.

Taro was unhappy with his performance in the playoffs that had just concluded. He opted to stay in the United States for an extended period, in order to work out with his friend Danny. The two had become quite close over their first three years in the league, and had become quite the dynamic pair on the ice.

In those early days, Taro would spend a lot of time on his own during the off-season. He preferred to read a lot, immersing himself in English books to learn the language better. He wasn't much of a social person in Buffalo either. On occasion, he would venture out on his own, or with a small group of teammates. But he generally preferred to stay at home a lot of the time. Danny Gare was one of the few people that Taro would go anywhere with for social outings in the off-season. Gare would try and set up Taro with the occasional woman, but Taro asked him to stop, saying that he wasn't very interested in dating at that point. His teammates recall:

> "During the season, Taro would go with the team for a post-game drink or two. He would stay long enough to be social, then leave. It was clear that he wasn't into the social scene though. That's too bad, because I thought that once he broke through that shyness of his, he would really take off on the ice. The two do go hand in hand. Success in one can lead to more confidence in the other. Taro just wasn't interested in being a social butterfly. I'm sure he was still missing his home country. His English was improving, but he still would stumble over the right phrase sometimes, and I think he worried that a woman might laugh at him if he said something the wrong way.

As his fourth season approached, Taro was more confident than ever that he was about to break through to the next level.

1977-78 SEASON

Taro's fourth season was a combination of a step forward, and a step backward. He moved forward in that he played all 80 games again, creating an impressive streak of 320 straight games played. It was a step backward, though, in that his production dropped from last season's personal best of 30 goals, down to just 20 goals. However, that was balanced with an increase in assists, as Taro became more of a playmaker, notching a career high of 42 assists. The Sabres, as a team, were definitely a beneficiary of that change in production. Taro had created a reputation for setting up teammates, as well as a keen eye when running a power play unit. He would often play on the blue line, taking the spot of one defenseman. With slick passing, and an excellent game sense, he would direct his teammates into position and send the puck their way. Even if he didn't ultimately get credit on the score sheet for power play work, he was always appreciated for his initial set-up work.

The team would get past the preliminary round in the playoffs again, but would fall to Philadelphia in five games. Taro had yet to find playoff success on the score sheet. His rookie season had been one with promise, but inexperience held him back. Now that he had the experience, he was being shut down by the opposition on a regular basis. It was a reputation that was only partially deserved. His teammates consistently gave him credit for his on-ice performance, but Taro always felt that he wasn't pulling his own weight.

When the team failed to even make it past the preliminary round in the 1978-79 playoffs, Taro knew that the situation in Buffalo was going to change. That season, his fifth, was another success during the regular season. He proved that he was a very capable player, scoring 25 goals and assisting on 33 others for a total of 58 points. He also was gaining a reputation as a gentlemanly player, winning that award for the first time with just 16 penalty minutes.

A lot of questions began to swirl around Taro about his ability to play, and succeed in the playoffs. Taro would, of course, work harder than ever to change this perception.

The 1979-80 season would bring a lot of changes to the NHL. First, four teams from the disbanded World Hockey Association, the WHA, would join the league. Edmonton, Winnipeg, New England (soon to be renamed Hartford) and Quebec. Now, 21 teams filled out the NHL. This season also marked the NHL debut of a young kid named Wayne Gretzky, the much heralded rookie superstar. While Gretzky would with the MVP, he would lose the leading scorer title, even though he tied in total points. Los Angeles had a forward that would win by the fact that he scored two more goals than Gretzky.

Also notable that season was the 35-game undefeated streak by the Philadelphia. The first win came on October 14th, and their final win on January 6th, against Taro's Buffalo club. One final note, the NHL president mandated helmets for all NHL players, with the exception of any player who signed a contract before June 1st, 1979. Taro had worn a helmet during his entire career so far, and stated that he was in favor of all players wearing helmets for better safety. He recalls:

> "The NHL front office decided that everyone on the league, all the players, should start wearing helmets for protection. I wore my helmet from day one and was thankful that I had. I tried out a little Japanese flag on the sides of mine, but the Sabres wouldn't allow it. They said it went against league rules."

Buffalo would win their division this season, beating out Boston for the title. Taro would set a new personal high in assists, putting up 58 assists along with a career high 80 points.

The Sabres won their division during the season, and would continue a strong run into the playoffs as well. They dispatched Vancouver and Chicago fairly easily, before running into the eventual NHL champion in New York. It was a hard fought series against their New York rivals. Many experts pointed to the

Game 2 double-overtime loss by Buffalo as a point where Taro's club began to fall apart, but it was probably Game 3, in which New York won the game by a 7-4 score that could have demoralized Buffalo the worst. Ironically, that game did the opposite, and they would reverse that score, beating New York in their own building by the identical 7-4 score.

Unfortunately, that was the last game that Buffalo would win in the series, falling to New York in six games.

Taro would finally break out of his playoff slump, scoring seven goals, along with five assists, all the way through the post-season. It would be a fitting finish to his second NHL contract, and would likely play a part in the off- season negotiations. Taro was ready to break out into the upper echelon of the NHL, but was the management in Buffalo ready for him to break out?

That was the big question that had to be answered.

The summer of 1980 was a long one for Taro. He wanted to stay in Buffalo, but wasn't sure that the Sabres were going to resign him to a long-term deal. He finally decided to go into the negotiations looking for a two-year deal. This was tossed around with team officials off and on for nearly three days before a decision would be reached. Taro would get a one-year deal, and nothing else. There was talk that the team had considered trading him somewhere out west, where they would only see him once or twice a year. The idea of playing somewhere other than Buffalo was a thought that Taro was slowly coming to grips with, and he let it be known that he would be open to a trade, if the right team was interested. He was firmly rebuked, being told, quite abruptly, he wouldn't have much say in the manner. He wasn't surprised, and accepted his fate, wherever he would land. Would he finish the next season with Buffalo, or would he be traded? That was a big question hovering over him as he went to training camp. A teammate recalls:

> "The night before the season started, Taro told me that the team had indicated that he might be up for a trade during the season. He didn't know what to think of that. I think it bothered him a great deal, even though he wouldn't show it. All I could do was to reassure him that wherever he landed, I would be there if he needed a friend. He was very pleased to hear that, and I think it helped settle him down."

Rumors of a trade followed Taro for much of the early part of the season. Those rumors didn't seem to slow him down a lot, as he came out of the gate on fire. He scored 14 goals in the first half of the season, just missing out on an All-Star berth. His offensive explosion naturally led to expanded trade rumors.

As the season progressed, Taro became much more aware

that he was on the trading block. He refused to show it on the ice. His performance was never better, and beyond reproach. If the persistent rumors were true, Taro Tsujimoto was either oblivious or just blocking it out. Either way, anyone watching him from the stands wouldn't know. It just wasn't Taro's style to let something like that affect his play on the ice.

Sure enough, just before the trade deadline, Taro would find himself moving out of Buffalo. While he hated to leave his teammates and friends, he would be fortunate to find himself in a position where he would be able to help lead a fairly young team. Again, a teammate recalls the conversation:

> "Taro came to me on the plane ride back to Buffalo right before the trade deadline. He said that he was being traded. When I asked him where he was going, he told me that he had been traded to Edmonton. It took him three tries to pronounce the city. I tried not to laugh. I reminded him that I was only a phone call away if he needed a friend. We also promised to get together in the off-season, and spend some time together."

Taro was about to take a journey to Edmonton. What would happen there, over the next few years, would change Taro forever, and the league as well.

The day Taro joined his new team in Edmonton, he was greeted by several players. Taro recalls:

> "I was surprised to see so many of my teammates meeting me at the airport. One of them had even taken the time to get my name spelled out, in Japanese, on a large piece of cardboard. They really wanted me to feel comfortable with the team from the very beginning. Arrangements for me to stay with one of the guys in town for a few weeks were already in place. Wayne asked if I wanted to try playing wing with him during practice a few times, just to see what happened. I was blown away. Here was a big name star, asking me to play on his line. Of course, I said yes. It started out that way in practice, and soon would develop in game action."

Yes, that's right. "The Great One," Wayne himself wanted to try Taro as a winger with him. It was going to be an experiment at times, something tried primarily on the power play, but it worked. Taro would play on the blue line, directing the power play unit and trying to set up his teammates. Many of the players were impressed by their new teammate. When you stop and look at it, it's understandable. Taro was finishing up his seventh season, while many of the Oilers had only been playing in the NHL for one or two seasons. Taro was a grizzled vet by league standards.

Taro would finish the season with a combined 31 goals, and a total of 72 points overall. It was a bit difficult to see that Buffalo finished 5th overall in the league, while Edmonton would come in 14th. Worse yet, Edmonton had to face a very strong Montreal club.

Taro's first thought was to predict that Edmonton would win the series. Flat out, no doubts in his mind, the Oilers would win. He took it for granted, and informed the rest of the team that they would be winning. That's probably the first time that his teammates began to think of him as a true dressing room leader.

Taro's years of experience would shine in the 1981 post-season. Apparently, someone forgot to tell the young Oilers that they weren't supposed to have much chance against the much more experienced Montreal club.

Taro had other ideas. He would score four goals in the Montreal series, two of them game winners. He also played a lot of power play time. Edmonton would go on to sweep Montreal in three straight games, shocking the entire NHL to the core. The Oilers didn't have a lot of time to enjoy their taste of victory, as they would earn a shot at the defending champions. Not knowing any better, and feeling invincible, they took the champs to six grueling games before falling. Again, the champs had bested Taro in the playoffs. He was tired of seeing them celebrating after a series win.

By the way, Taro had done so well on the wing with Wayne, that he moved to that position almost exclusively after that season.

As the off-season passed, several things happened for Taro. First, he was rewarded with a 5-year contract extension. The Oilers wanted him to stay for several years. They liked his game, his attitude, and most importantly, his leadership.

While Taro wouldn't wear a leadership letter on his sweater for the immediate future, it was becoming obvious that he was developing into a leader. His experience was a big bonus to a young Edmonton club, and Wayne made sure that everyone in the dressing room knew it, too.

In May, while the Finals were being successfully defended by New York, Taro went out with several of his Edmonton teammates to go hang out at a local club. The players were treated almost like living legends, and fans came up to them asking for autographs, and asking to buy them drinks.

This was something new for Taro. He hadn't been out nearly as much in Buffalo, instead preferring to stay at home for the most part, or go out quietly and remain anonymous. Unfortunately for him, it was nearly impossible to go out anywhere in

Buffalo due to his success.

Now, feeling much more confident with his much more outgoing teammates in Edmonton, he seemed to relish the attention. One woman in particular caught his eye. She was nearly as tall as Taro, a full-figured redhead who was sporting an Edmonton shirt that evening. She was one person with whom Taro found a connection. Her name was Taylor Morris. She knew hockey inside and out. Her attitude was positively incredible, and helped put Taro at ease from the beginning. The two talked for almost two hours before the hockey players announced, to the dismay of their adoring fans, that they were heading out for the night. Taylor passed her phone number to Taro as he was getting up to leave. He tried to tell her that he wasn't all that interested in dating at that point, being so new in town. Taylor wouldn't hear of it, and asked him to call her in the next couple of days. She was interested. Taro recalls:

> "Taylor was a lot different from the women I met in Buffalo. Back in Buffalo, the women just wanted to hang out with the players and be seen. I went out with a couple of women and all they wanted to do was parade me past their friends.
>
> Taylor was different. She knew she wasn't built like the average woman. She didn't act like most of the women I met that first night. But when we started

talking, she had a lot more personality and character. That's why I finally decided to call her the next day. I weighed it for the night, and even asked one of the guys what I should do. He suggested that I call her and see what happened. After all, nothing ventured, nothing gained. So I called her. As it turns out, it was the right choice. After I went home, I was asked by my roommate if I was going to call her. I figured it was worth a chance, so I did."

It would be a decision that would ultimately change the lives of both of them.

Taro had finally found a woman he was able to be comfortable with, and soon he and Taylor would become quite the item over the summer. But he made it clear that he was a hockey player first, and he had to work out during the summer to stay in shape for the upcoming season. Taylor worked at an office close to the arena as an executive assistant. After a few dates, Taro signed a puck for her, and she put it on display at her desk. Taro recalls:

"After I gave Taylor that puck, she changed a little bit. I think it brought us closer together. She did say that her co-workers were giving her a bad time about dating a hockey player, but she didn't care. Several of my teammates were also giving me a bad time. I think they thought I could do better, find a better looking woman. But it was Wayne who told me that if I was happy, then I should pursue happiness.

Wayne had signed a puck for me when I first joined the team. I have that puck on the mantle at home, and it will remain a cherished reminder of all the advice he gave me when I started out with the team."

With a little guidance from Taylor, Taro would find a modest apartment just a short distance away from the arena. He moved in his new home in July, and settled quickly. Many of his Edmonton teammates would help "break it in" with a big party. Taylor was a regular fixture at his place as well. The two were becoming quite the pair, and Taro was on cloud nine as training camp drew close. Taylor, of course, would take a back seat to the hockey season. She wouldn't allow herself to be a distraction for Taro. She wanted him to be ready for a full season in Edmonton.

As the season started, Taro continued to wear number 74, the number he had worn throughout his career in Buffalo. He was looking forward to a full year in Edmonton, and seeing what he could accomplish with Edmonton. With Wayne leading the way, life was about to take off.

Chapter 4
1981-82 season

The 1981-82 season started out with a bang. The team would win 9 of their first 13 games. Taro would score six goals in that time period. He was also responsible for setting up five more. With the man advantage, Taro would man the blue-line, paired with one of Edmonton's finest defensemen. It was almost unfair to the rest of the league, though. Taro tended to stay back on the blue-line, while his partner was free to roam the offensive zone more often.

On October 31st, 1981, Taro sent three passes to Wayne, which were buried for his 7th career hat trick. Wayne would eventually finish the game with his second career four-goal game. A month later, Taro was instrumental in setting up three of Wayne's four goals, his 3rd four-goal game. Taro recalls that things were becoming a lot of fun:

"Once I arrived in Edmonton, and started playing

a full season, I found a new love of the game. These young players had all sorts of energy and a love of the game that I had never seen to this point. It was fun to go to the arena every night. I found that I was much more eager to play each night also. Knowing that Taylor was keeping track of the games as well probably helped. I wanted to succeed on the ice to show her that I was worthy of wearing the uniform.

She would come over a couple times a week, when the schedule allowed, and we would have dinner together, or sometimes we would just sit on the couch and talk. We had a lot to share, and we were eager to get to know each other."

By the end of November, Taro had not only earned the respect of every single player and coach in the Edmonton dressing room, but he was earning the adoration of all the Edmonton fans. The "Taro Says..." signs, that had been so popular in Buffalo, were starting to show up in Edmonton, along with shirts and buttons. Taro even spent part of an afternoon signing buttons for the fans, as well as other items that would eventually be sold at the team store as well. No one knows how it transferred from Buffalo to Edmonton, but it caught on like wildfire.

Taro celebrated a slightly late Christmas, on December

27th, by setting up two of Wayne's goals, on his 3rd four goal game of the season, and 4th of his career. Wayne had been on a tear in the beginning of the season, and was approaching a landmark faster than ever. It wasn't going to be a question of whether he would get 50 goals in the season, it was going to be how fast he would do it.

Taro and Taylor celebrated the New Year a day early at the game on December 30th. Taro would feed Wayne four assists, helping set up what would eventually become his 50th goal of the year in an unheard of, record-breaking 39 games. It would be Wayne's 11th hat trick, and 2nd career five goal game. Taro recalls:

> "During the first part of the season, I found a connection with Wayne, and played often on the wing with him. He told me not to worry if I missed a pass or two. I was just to put it near him, and he would take care of the rest. Well, I found it easy to put the puck right on his stick, and sure enough, he would almost always bury the shots. I was instrumental in helping him to many milestones. In fact, I had the primary assist on his 50th goal. He made sure that everyone knew I had passed it to him. A few days later, he gave Taylor and I a signed and framed jersey. On the numbers, he had written 'To Taro, thanks for all your help on the ice.' It's

up on the wall in the living room. He also gave Taylor one of my game-worn jerseys, telling her that I was too shy to give her a present that significant. I know that he wasn't trying to embarrass me, but it did just that for a short time. Wayne had, by this time, become more than a teammate, he was a close friend."

Yes, even with his success in Edmonton, Taro was still quite shy around Taylor. She was good for him, though. He was learning to express himself a lot more since meeting her.

While Taro wasn't named to the All-Star game, he was a key part of the Oilers to that point, a very important player. None other than Wayne agreed. Taro recalls a few words of wisdom from the Great One:

"Taro was quite a player. I knew that he was destined to be a great player. All he needed was the right system to play in, and Edmonton was a team that actively encouraged the fast end-to-end rushes that Taro was best at. He developed his on-ice vision with a little help from me, but he already had the talent. I just helped him hone his skills a little better."

Many times, Taro would take off up the ice, cut to one

side or the other just inside the offensive blue line, and slowly down the boards, watching to see what developed. With help from Wayne, Taro was becoming one of the best playmakers in the league.

Taro heard from his friend Danny around Christmas time. Danny had been traded from Buffalo to Detroit. While Danny was upbeat about the trade, he knew it would pretty much destroy any chance of a deep playoff run anytime soon. Detroit wasn't as good as they had been many years ago, and now had a reputation for finishing near the bottom of their division. Taro tried to console his friend. Ironically, the student, Taro, was now the teacher.

During the All-Star break, Taro and Taylor decided to drive off to visit her parents in Calgary. It was the first time that he met Rick and Nancy. Apparently Taylor had forgotten to tell her boyfriend that her parents were die-hard fans of Edmonton's number one rival, Calgary. Taylor recalls:

> "I never thought much of the fact that my parents were Flames fans. I was an Edmonton fan, obviously. But since I didn't talk to my parents very often, we usually didn't take a lot of time to talk about hockey. It's not that we didn't get along, it was a case of all of us being busy people and not having a lot of time to just

sit around on the phone. Besides, if I got started with Mom, I would end up talking for thirty minutes or so. Taro was wearing his team hat as we pulled up, and Dad gave him a bad time right away about it. Nothing terribly serious, but I think Dad just wanted to make a point. We got past it quick enough, though. I really think, looking back on it, that having hockey as a common interest helped break the ice with Dad. Taro was comfortable around him fairly quickly, and that really surprised me.

My parents asked Taro a lot of things about his life, and his experiences. It was clear that they were testing him also. I know Mom, in particular, wanted to make sure of his intentions. Mom suggested that I come up to Calgary and watch a game. I told her that, if I went, I would be wearing my own gear, and cheering for my boyfriend. They grudgingly agreed to disagree with me on that one. I think they secretly liked the idea of me dating an NHL star, but they weren't going to show it just yet."

As it turned out, Taylor had conveniently left out the fact that her parents were Calgary fans, just to see what they thought of Taro. As it turned out, they weren't too concerned about it.

Aside from some good natured grief every so often, it didn't come up all that often.

It was probably fate that had Taro setting up some of Wayne's records. He assisted on the goal that gave Wayne his 165th point of the year, a new NHL record. Taro would score a goal, assisted by Wayne, that gave Wayne the record for assists in a season.

Taro also assisted on Wayne's 77th goal, and his 90th goal, both records. Wayne would finish the year with 92 goals, still a league record, and one that likely won't ever be broken.

For the year, Taro would finish with 35 goals, and a very impressive personal record of 78 assists. He would also set personal high scores with 12 power play goals, and 5 short handed goals. Taro also continued his consecutive games streak, stretching it to 642 games.

Career-wise, Taro had scored his 200th career goal, a milestone that no one had ever expected. Now, looking back at his performance to this point, it seemed only natural.

As Taro and his teammates geared up for the playoffs, they prepared to face Los Angeles. It wasn't expected to be a difficult series, but after the first two games, the series was tied. Taro was shut down in the first two games, only recording one assist. But, things were about to get worse for Edmonton.

In Game 3, down south in Los Angeles, Edmonton took

a 5-0 lead heading into the third period. Most hockey fans would have guessed it was over. But in a game that would be known as "the Miracle on Manchester," the home team would storm back for 5 goals in the third period, finishing off the game with an overtime winner, to take a 2-1 series lead. While Edmonton would tie the series in Game 4, Los Angeles would eliminate their pesky opponent in Game 5. It was a huge shock for the hockey world, and the city of Edmonton. The players were stunned, the coaches were surprised, and no one really knew what to do after that upset.

For days, Taro was down and depressed. He knew that his lackluster performance had been one of many keys to the failure in the playoffs. While players like Wayne took a lot of the blame, Taro took it upon himself to try and deflect the targets away from his super-star teammate. This was the first time he had been on a team that was shocked in the playoffs. It was a feeling he wasn't used to, and it was going to take some time for him to recover.

Looking back at the season, Taro had reached new career highs with 35 goals and 113 points. He was pleased with those accomplishments. But he was disappointed that the playoffs came to such an abrupt end.

At the suggestion of a couple of his teammates, as well as his friend Danny, Taro took Taylor on a short vacation. They decided to go to Hawaii for a few days, to get away from the spotlight. The two lovebirds would find happiness by the boatload on the islands. Taylor wasn't used to such an extravagance, and Taro took every opportunity to shower love and attention on his girlfriend. They celebrated one full year together on their last day in Hawaii.

They would both return well-tanned, and fully refreshed. While the idea of a serious relationship had initially seemed foreign to Taro since he had arrived in North America, he was certainly making up for lost time. He seemed to have found his soul-mate in Taylor. She, at the same time, had found someone who loved her for who she was. Taylor recalls:

"I remember walking along the beach in Hawaii with Taro. We would walk past people while holding hands, and he didn't care a single bit that others would look at us and stare. I had asked him, before we left, if I should even bother bringing a swimsuit. He insisted that I do so, even taking me out to get something new the day we arrived in Honolulu. He told me, simply, that we were going to spend a lot of time at the beach, and I should be ready to enjoy the beach.

I've never been in a relationship with a man that cared so much about me. Taro was an amazing person to find, and I doubt I would ever find someone like him again. He insisted that we fly first class, so I would have a more comfortable seat on the airplane. He's so thoughtful like that. He's always putting me first in our relationship. I'm hoping that our second year together is even better than the first.

Oh! One more thing. Our last night in Hawaii, he bought me a necklace. All I know is that it looks amazing when I wear it. He says that someday, he's going to get me a Championship ring, just like the players get. Well, after he wins one, of course. That way, I can be his championship girl. I guess that gives a whole new meaning to trophy girlfriend, right? How did I get so lucky finding him? I don't know, but I know better than to question reality. He's the most amazing guy in the world, and he's all mine!"

It's clear that Taylor and Taro were attached at the hip. He was practically glowing when he arrived at training camp in the fall, for two reasons. First, he was prepared to break through to the next level, and try to become a major star on a team that was rapidly developing stars.

Second, on a much more personal level, he had big news. Taylor was pregnant, and Taro decided to propose right away.

Naturally, she accepted, and they set about preparing themselves for a wedding in the near future. They both knew it would have to wait until the off season. That meant that Taylor was going to have the baby before the wedding. Taylor recalls:

"I was so nervous when I sat Taro down to tell him the big news. It was in the evening, after dinner. I thought if we were both relaxed it might go easier. I had been to see the doctor because I wasn't feeling well, and she gave me the news. Now, I had to go tell my boyfriend.

I finally managed to tell him after several minutes of hesitation. He was pleased, almost joyous. I asked him what he thought about becoming a parent. He promptly got down on one knee and asked me to marry him right then and there. Of course, I said yes. He promised to take me out the next day and buy me a ring to make it official. I told him to take his time with the ring. We had to get busy planning to be parents and to get married. It was going to be a busy season. My doctor was predicting a due date in mid-March. I was actually relieved when she said that, because it meant that the baby would have arrived before the playoffs started. I wanted Taro to be totally focused on hockey when the playoffs came around.

Fortunately, I had been at my office position for nearly four years, and had some vacation time coming up. I would be able to use that in the near future as things progressed. They also had given me a rather sizable raise just after we got back from Hawaii. That would help as well.

I just can't say enough about Taro. He was such a pillar in my life at that point, and it looked like he was going to be around for the long-term as well."

1982-83 SEASON

The team began the season with the goal of making it deep into the playoffs, and hopefully challenging for the championship. However, after the first two months of the season, they were just barely above .500 and treading water in the middle of the division.

December was the key, and the team turned itself around and took off with gusto. After losing 9 games in the first two months of the year, they would lose just 11 more the rest of the year. It would come as no surprise to anyone familiar with Edmonton that when Taro got himself back on track, the entire team seemed to be jump started into action.

They had just completed a win in Hartford in early March and were on their way back when Taylor went into labor. Her mother, who had driven from Calgary to stay with her for the past two weeks, drove her to the hospital. The team was barely back in town, and Taro was met at the airport by front office staff. His gear was hauled off to the arena for him, and he grabbed his suitcase and was driven straight to the hospital. Within hours, Taylor gave birth to twins, a girl named Kimberly, and a boy named Wayne. Taro had insisted that their son would be named after his hockey hero, Wayne. Taylor agreed completely with that choice. Taro recalls:

"Taylor is quite a woman. Our daughter was born first. Kimberly has the red hair, just like Taylor. My son, Wayne, also had red hair. I told Wayne that I was naming my son after him and he was visibly emotional about that choice.

My teammates gave us several presents for the two children, but none more impressive than the beginning of a college fund for them, with a total of nearly five thousand dollars to start."

Taylor remembers from her perspective:

"I was a bit worried that Taro wouldn't be back from his road trip when Mom and I were going to the hospital. Mom was extremely helpful in the early stages of my stay at the hospital, but once Taro arrived, she moved into the background.

Taro was such a trooper the entire time. I knew he would be, but I still wondered how he would act after a long road trip. I didn't need to worry, because he was on top of things, just the way we had rehearsed.

After the babies had both arrived, we were holding them for a few minutes. Taro and I had already agreed on names, but it was our first chance to call them by their names. I know that Taro was particularly pleased in naming our son after his teammate, Wayne. We needed about two seconds to agree on that choice. I named our daughter, Kimberly. It was a name that came from my family, and I thought it sounded nice. Taro agreed, and that was that."

Again, Wayne was the big star, shining brightly on the way to 196 points overall on the year. The team would tie a record with four 100-point scorers on the year. Taro would fall just short of 100 points that year, and missed out on a chance to be part of a new league record. He would score 31 goals, and finish the year with 99 points.

The playoffs beckoned, and in the first round, Edmonton swept Winnipeg in 3 straight games. This propelled Edmonton into the first ever "Battle of Alberta" against their rivals in Calgary. While Taro was playing for Edmonton, his fiancee Taylor was at home with the new kids, cheering for her team. Her dad was able to attend Game 2 in Edmonton, thanks to Taro's efforts. Ultimately, Edmonton would make short work of Calgary, dispatching them in 5 quick games. This was followed by a sweep of Chicago, sending the Oilers to the Stanley Cup Finals. Unfortunately, Edmonton would get swept in 4 straight games by New

York, who would win their 4th straight Championship.

While Taro was disappointed in losing the Finals, he was pleased that his team had made it that far. It was the first trip to the Finals, and this young team learned a lot of lessons the hard way, watching what New York had done.

It is said that a person must crawl, then stumble as they learn to walk. In the same vein, the players from Edmonton were learning. They had finally made it to the Finals, but learned a very valuable lesson in how to finish a championship. These lessons would come into play in the coming seasons.

Meanwhile, a much shorter off-season loomed, and a busy one at that. Taro and Taylor were finalizing plans to get married. The big day was scheduled in mid-July, and the twins were, by this point, four months old. Taylor's parents and other relatives were tasked to help with the twins. Most of the players, as well as many of the coaches and upper office staff were present as well. Wayne, Mark and one other player would be the best men, and stand beside Taro at the altar. Taro's father was able to fly in from Japan to be part of the ceremony, the first time that he had ever flown to Edmonton. It was also the first meeting between him and Taylor's parents. Taylor recalls:

"I remember meeting Taro's father the night before the wedding. He was very formal. I really couldn't tell

if he approved of me or not at first. After awhile, he seemed to relax and accept me. I think a lot of the issue at stake was that we already had kids, before getting married. Believe me, we hadn't exactly planned on things happening this way. But, sometimes you just have to go with the flow.

Taro got the kids cute little onesies. For Kimberly, her's is pink and says 'Taro says, I'm Daddy's girl.' For Wayne, his is blue and says 'Taro says, I'm Daddy's boy.'

I already told Taro that we're saving those for the future, even after they grow out of them. I want to frame them and put them on the wall. Eventually, the kids can have them as presents from their hockey-playing dad."

It was a magical day for everyone. Taylor was gorgeous in her bridal gown, and Taro looked stellar in his suit. The twins were dressed up in a style that can only be described as baby formal. A wonderful day for everyone involved. After the magical words were spoken, Taro and Taylor had their first kiss as a married couple, and headed down the aisle. They would change for the reception, and enjoy the party into the evening. Taro recalls the ceremony:

"Taylor looked absolutely wonderful. It was a real treat to see her in the wedding dress. She had taken great steps to make sure that I never saw it before the wedding, and believe me, it was worth it.

Wayne and two of the players stood with me, and a number of other guys from the team were there as well. Danny flew in from Detroit at the last minute to be with us as well. That was a real treat."

While Taylor's parents took care of the twins, Taro and Taylor spent their honeymoon in Tokyo, courtesy of Hiro. Taylor learned all about Taro's youth, and they spent a wonderful six days in the "Land of the Rising Sun." Taylor acquired a liking for sushi. She also discovered that Taro was a national hero. They would be hounded by the press and the general public wherever they went. If they went to a restaurant, they would end up nestled into a back booth, hiding from the endless cameras. Taro would spend a lot of time signing pictures, hockey pucks, almost anything that people would shove in front of him. One young woman, who barely looked eighteen, pushed her way in front of Taro, pulled up her sweater, and insisted that he sign her cleavage. Insanity ruled that day. It was difficult at times, finding privacy with the hoopla surrounding them. It was very much a lesson in culture shock. Never in her dreams did she think she'd be this close to utter chaos on a regular basis. She recalls:

> "The first day in Tokyo, we were hounded almost to the point of harassed by people trying to get Taro's autograph. I didn't know what to say, and tried to stay out of the way. Outside one place, a mob of people pushed toward us, and I got separated from Taro for almost an hour. I was scared for some time, being alone in a strange country. Fortunately, a policeman helped me find a safe place to sit, and even got me a drink while I waited. He then reunited me with Taro after helping shoo away a crowd of people. It got to where we had to have an escort with us. I have never been so thankful to not have the kids with me."

The trip to Tokyo was exactly what Taro needed to re-focus on hockey and his life with Taylor and his family. As training camp drew close, he was focused on one goal; winning a championship and raising the cherished trophy over his head like so many before him.

1983-84 Season

The season started off red-hot out of the gates. Taro and his teammates were winning almost everything, 39 of their first 53 games to be exact. Wayne started the season equally strong, with an NHL-record streak with at least one point in his first fifty-one games. On November 6th, Taro would set up two of Wayne's four goals, his 5th four goal game of his career to that point. Taro continued his set-up work, notching two more assists on the 20th hat-trick of Wayne's career on November 12th.

But it was on November 19th that the league truly got notice of Taro's abilities. It would be a slightly late present, just three days after his 28th birthday. Taylor's parents were in town, and they accompanied Taylor, with the twins, to the game that night. Taro had managed to get excellent seats for the family, and they settled in to watch their team take on New Jersey. By the end of the night, Taro would cement his place in Edmonton history.

Taro would set up a rookie defenseman, in his NHL debut, for his first career goal during the game. The goalie would notch an assist as Wayne achieved career hat trick number 21. Taro also had two assists in that landmark. But Taro would also add four more assists, as "The Fabulous Finn" would score both his sixth hat trick and his very first five-goal game in the NHL. This gave Taro six assists on the night, a single-game personal and career record. While some focused on Wayne's latest hat trick, or the first five-goal game by Taro's Finnish teammate, most of the team was talking about Taro and his achievement. No doubt, Taylor was beside herself with her husband's performance. She recalls:

> "I have told him many times that it's better to give than receive. I think he took me seriously that night. Of course, I was cheering with every Oilers goal that was scored, but I was loudest when Taro's name was announced. My parents were cheering loudly as well. They may have been Calgary fans at heart, but I think Taro was winning them over that night.
>
> I know that he was exhausted by the time he finally got out of the dressing room after the game. But, I have never seen such a huge smile like the one he wore when he finally saw me after the game. He handed me his jersey, and asked me to wear it in the future. He signed the numbers 'To Taylor, thanks for all six of my assists tonight.' It's got the date on it too, so we both know when he made that wonderful record."

Almost one month later, Taro would help Wayne out once again, adding two assists on his latest hat trick, number 22.

The Legend of Taro Tsujimoto

Taro had a richly deserved reputation now as a set-up man for Edmonton. He enjoyed the attention, but still preferred to stay on the perimeter and the edges, letting the rest of the team score the goals, and he picked up the assists.

In February, in back-to-back games, Taro would earn six assists as Wayne scored four goals in each game. It was almost a constant mantra for the team. Taro sets 'em up, "The Great One" finishes. Taro would go on to finish with career highs in assists and total points. It was also his fourth consecutive 30 goal season, and fifth overall.

Taro and company swept Winnipeg in three straight games in the opening round of the playoffs, then would face Calgary in a surprisingly tough series. Taylor would make the drive, with the twins, to Calgary for Games 3 and 4. She and her parents would be in attendance to watch as Taro led the way to a win in both of those games. Taro was able to pull off a surprise for Taylor's parents. While history does not reveal the methods that he used, Taro was able to get signed, game-worn jerseys, one red, one white, for both of them from one of Calgary's players, a future NHL Hall of Fame. They were speechless, of course, but accepted. Taylor recalls:

"Taro has never told me the story of the Flames jerseys. All he has ever said was that he managed to

talk with the player in question, and was able to get two game-worn jerseys signed for my parents. I suspect that Taro traded one of his jerseys, but I've never heard anything to confirm or deny that tale. All I know is that my parents were on cloud nine after receiving them. Dad was like a big kid, bouncing around his house wearing the jersey. Mom could barely contain her excitement as well. Sometimes, it pays to have the right people in the right places."

However it happened, Taro was a hero to his wife and her parents. Let's face it, that's the best way to get ahead in life. If the wife is happy, then everyone at home is happy.

The Calgary series went the full seven games before Edmonton finally put them away. Edmonton moved on to the conference championship, and faced off with Minnesota. While only one game was decided by more than one goal, the series itself wasn't really in doubt. Edmonton would sweep Minnesota and proceed back to the Stanley Cup Finals. Once again, they would face New York , who was in the midst of their "Drive for Five."

With a week between the end of the previous series and the beginning of the Finals, Taro, and the rest of the club, allowed themselves a little downtime. Taro stayed at home with his family. The twins were now starting to walk and try their hand at talking, and Taro was often busy following one or both of them around the house. When Taylor's parents arrived in Edmonton ahead of the Finals, Taylor gave them some surprising news. She was expecting again.

Taro managed to get tickets for Taylor's parents for Games 3 and 4. He also had assurances from several teammates that, should the series go a fifth game, he would have tickets for that game as well.

As the teams gathered on Long Island for the first two games, the Oilers found themselves more determined than ever to make sure they left New York with at least a split of the two games. Edmonton would shut out New York in Game One, shocking all of the NHL. However, reality came back with a vengeance badly in Game Two as New York torched Edmonton for six goals, and it was off to Alberta for the next three games. If necessary, games six and seven would be back in New York, but none of Edmonton's squad wanted anything other than to end the series at home. Taro recalls:

> "I made a statement on the plane ride back to Edmonton. Basically, I told everyone that we had lost our last game in the Finals, and we would sweep the rest of the games. Some of the players weren't sure about that, but I know some of the veterans thought I was doing

the right thing."

Taro undoubtedly knew what he was doing, instilling confidence in his teammates. Arriving back in Edmonton, the entire team was focused on just one thing, taking a stand as champions.

Game Three finally arrived, and Taro, Wayne and the rest of the roster came out flying. While defense had been a hallmark of New York's four titles, Edmonton finally broke through and were able to show what they could do. New York scored only two goals, while Wayne, Taro, Mark and the rest of the team lit them up for seven goals, and a lead in the series. Game Four was the same thing, and an identical 7-2 final score in Game Four left Edmonton just one game away from their first title.

May 18th was an off day. The team held a light skate in the morning, and the rest of the day was left to the individuals. Taro spent the afternoon at home, with Taylor, the twins and her parents. Little Kimberly and Wayne were wobbling around the house, learning to walk, to the delight of Taro and Taylor. It was a low key evening. Taro went to bed early, in hopes of getting some rest before what was, to this point, the biggest game of his life.

May 19th, 1984 dawned brightly in Edmonton. The entire city had Stanley fever, the Stanley Cup that is. Taro played with the twins in the morning. He recalls:

"Taylor tried to keep everyone away from me as much as possible those last couple of days. She wanted me to be focused on the games and not so much on life at home. Her parents helped keep an eye on the kids as well. However, knowing that she was almost three months pregnant, I wanted to do as much as I could to help take some of the load off her shoulders. It made for some funny moments."

Taro made breakfast that fateful morning, and the family discussed the upcoming game while they ate. The conversation was relatively light, and an effort was made not to talk about hockey too much.

Taro was one of the first players to arrive at the ice rink. He went for a short run around the parking lot before heading inside to gather his gear. He brought a light pre-game meal of sushi, and relaxed with his food, dunking it liberally with wasabi every few seconds. Some of his teammates apparently weren't familiar with sushi, and seemed slightly put off by Taro's choice of food.

Everyone in the dressing room was ready a little too early, and nerves were readily visible. If Edmonton lost this game, they would head back to New York. If that happened, it was generally believed that they could lose the entire series. No one wanted to go back east.

Warm-ups went well, and in the pre-game speech, the coaching staff took it easy. Everyone knew how big this game was, they all knew who and what to watch for, so there wasn't a lot to say that hadn't been said already.

As the teams took the ice for the beginning of the game, Taro could feel the tension in the building. Everyone present was about to witness history.

The game was relatively close for awhile, but as it wore on, it became obvious that the younger club was starting to take control. When Taro broke free of a scramble at mid-rink and raced down to score a goal midway through the third period, the entire building exploded in delight. The crowd started chanting "Taro! Taro!" Edmonton would get their fifth goal of the game late in the third period, and would skate off with the victory. As the final horn sounded, the Edmonton bench emptied. Gear was thrown every which way, players leaped onto each other, and the building was screaming in happiness. Edmonton had done the unthinkable; in just their 5th year in the NHL, they had won their first Championship.

Mere days after the final game was played, the parade that was held in Edmonton was to be epic. Taro would ride in a convertible with none other than Wayne, holding the trophy. At the podium, Taro said a few words about hockey in Japan. He hoped that Japanese kids would see him playing in the NHL, and realize that it was possible to follow in his footsteps and play in the professional leagues. He recalls:

> "I was on cloud nine the day of the parade. As we rode through town, fans were cheering for all of us, but I saw a lot of 'Taro says...' signs along the route. I know that Taylor was watching at home with the twins, and I also know that she was very proud of me.
>
> We held a big party at the house in the evening a few days after the victory. The trophy was there, and I had a chance to get pictures of Taylor, the twins and I with the trophy. We even got pictures of each of the kids sitting in the top bowl on the Stanley Cup. Later that night, after everyone had left, the Stanley Cup was still at our house. I had promised to bring it back to the ice rink in the morning. I was personally hosting a skating party for a large group of kids."

Yes, the first thing Taro wanted to do after winning the trophy was to bring in a bunch of kids, have them go skating for an hour or two, and get a photo with the Stanley Cup. That's the sort of guy he was, and still is.

Chapter 5

In the off-season, Taro found himself much more in demand. He would appear on two sports radio shows and a television show as well. The growing sports cable network in the United States, ESPN, wanted to do a 30-minute feature on the first NHL player from Japan. Taro was interviewed extensively, plus some filming was done in Edmonton as he took the camera crew around town. Taylor was briefly interviewed as well. It was a lot of fun for both of them, and it certainly didn't hurt the legend of Taro one single bit. During the interview time, a surprise guess arrived. Danny had flown in from Detroit for the program. It was an emotional reunion, as the two hadn't seen each other outside of an ice rink for several years. Danny finally met Taylor, and see the twins as well. The two hockey players spent three days going all over Edmonton together before Danny had to return to Detroit. They vowed not to take so long before the next visit.

Oh, one more note: As promised, now that they had won the title, and the players would be getting their rings, Taro completed his promise to Taylor. He arranged for a replica ring to be made and fitted for her.

1984-85 Season

Edmonton started their title defense with an record 15 game unbeaten streak. Wayne was still number one on the ice, and the game tended to revolve around his considerable skills. On October 21st, a special announcement was made to commemorate Wayne's 400th game. Less than two weeks after Taro's birthday, he would have two assists on another hat trick by Wayne. On December 15th, Taro would score one goal, on which "The Great One" would record his 1,000 NHL point. Taro would return the favor with four assists as Wayne notched his 3rd career five-goal game. But that wasn't the only player that Taro was setting up during the season. He would have three assists the night their super-speedy star defenseman, Paul, notched his very first four-goal game.

Big news for the Tsujimoto family in late November. Taylor delivered twins again, on November 17th. This time, twin boys. Steve and Danny were born moments apart, and on the same night that Edmonton shut out Vancouver 7-0. Fittingly, Taro would score one goal and set up another. Taylor recalls:

> "I told Taro that he was going to go ahead and play, no matter what happened. My mom drove down from Calgary to stay with us for a month or so, and, when it

was time, she took me to the hospital. We were watching the game on the television in my room. I think I scared a couple of nurses when Taro scored, because I was cheering so loudly. Mom was a real trooper, and helped out a lot.

After the game was over, Taro raced to the hospital and had a chance to see his sons. He stayed in the room with me for the night, but because I had gone to sleep early, I only saw him when I woke up in the morning. I remember he had draped a very large blanket with the team logo over me. It was a small, sweet gesture.

We went to the nursery later in the morning, and Taro got to hold his newly born sons for the first time. Now, he's as manly as any athlete out there. But at that moment, holding his sons, he started to break down and cry. I didn't care, because it just made him human."

Taro recalls the same night from his perspective:

"I remember being told before the game that Taylor was in the hospital. I wasn't too worried, because her mom was in town. During the first intermission, Wayne asked me about her. I didn't know anything new. He asked if I would need a ride after the game. Think about that for a moment. The best player in the league, having another great game, no doubt he will be busy with interviews after the game. Instead of staying for an extended period of time to talk with the reporters, he made plans to cut it short and take care of me. Sure enough, after the game, Wayne talked to the press for just a few minutes before calling a halt to everything. He even told the reporters that he was driving me to the hospital, to see my sons being born. The reporters tried to catch up to me, but Wayne and a few other guys impressed on them that family business was more important.

I can't say enough good things about everyone on the team. I don't know how many other superstars would drop everything and drive another teammate to the hospital.

Even more impressive, Wayne came to the hospital the next day, to see Taylor and the boys. He only stayed a few minutes, but he wanted to convey his best wishes from everyone on the team. Taylor was blown away by Wayne's generosity. We've never forgotten that day."

But it was at the end of January that Taro was on fire. He

would help set up Wayne's 50th goal of the season, putting up all three assists as "The Great One" scored his 33rd hat trick. Three days later, Taro had two assists to help someone else on his latest hat trick. To top the week off, Taro would set up all three of another youngster's first hat trick goals. Eight assists in a 7-day span was very impressive, and it would get him noticed as one of the NHL's three stars of the week.

    The team would finish in first place, again, with 49 wins. It would be their fourth consecutive division title. As a personal note, Taro would finish with his fifth straight 30-goal season, and again, would top 100 points, finishing with 106 total. It as also his fourth straight season with at least 100 points. More impressive, Taro again played all 80 games in the season, giving him a consecutive games streak which stood at 882 by season's end. When Taro was traded from Buffalo to Edmonton, his first team had played two more games than Edmonton to that point, and Taro was able to get into the line-up fast enough to play those extra games. As a side note, Wayne would post his 3rd career 200-point game, a feat never seen before, and likely never to be seen again.

    They made short work of Los Angeles and Winnipeg in the first two rounds. Chicago was a little tougher, and the teams would split the first four games. But, in Game Five, Edmonton doubled up Chicago 10-5 at home, sending the series back to the Windy City for what would be a decisive blowout victory by the Canadian squad. . In those last two games alone, Taro would score twice, and notch six assists. That would send Taro to the Finals for the third straight year.

Although there were five days from the last game of the Chicago series until the Finals started, they would fly directly to Philadelphia, and settle in for a couple of days before the series began. This would allow everyone to reduce the travel time. Taro called home at least once a day to talk with Taylor, at least before the Finals began. Kimberly and Wayne were starting to talk a lot, and Taro loved speaking on the phone with them. Taylor would be bringing the entire family to Game Four, with a little assistance from her parents.

Edmonton stumbled in Game One, however, falling by a 4-1 score. They would bounce back for a 3-1 win in Game Two, and return home with the split. Taro had no goals, and only one assist in the first two games. He was disappointed in his performance, and vowed to pick it up as the series progressed.

Game Three was close, all the way to the third period, where Edmonton finally managed to pull ahead, and finally win the game by a single goal. Taro set up two of the team's four goals, and he began to feel better about his game. With a little help from a teammate, and that name has been lost to time, Taro was able to get tickets for Game Five as well for his family.

Taylor, all four of the kids, and her parents were at Game

Four on May 28th, and they all saw the Taro lead the way again. Taro scored once, and set up another goal. It was a typical performance to which Philadelphia did not seem to have answer. Once again, Edmonton was on the edge of winning the championship. This time, it was a repeat performance that was about to happen. That would set up a potential series-clinching game just two days later.

Taro approached the time off between games the same way that he had done so often during the playoffs; he would stay at home with the family. While Taylor had her parents in town for a few days, it was always nice to have Taro at home. Taylor recalls his absences:

> "Being a hockey player has got to be quite demanding. I know being a hockey wife is tough enough for me. Taro is gone for so much of the season, and with the team going deep into the playoffs, he's missing even more time than he would with other teams. I'm not complaining at all, not by any means. I know he loves having been in the Finals several times in his career. After the down times in Buffalo, I know he's enjoying the good times here.
>
> It's nice to have him at home between games. I miss him a lot when he's gone, that's for sure. But we both

knew this would be a challenge when we decided to get serious about each other, long before we got married. I knew I'd be raising kids on my own much of the time. I don't think either of us expected to be raising four kids, especially with them so close in age. Two pairs of twins was a challenge, that's for sure. But anytime Taro was home, he would take charge, and help out a lot. He insisted on sending me to bed many times and stay up with them while I got a nap. He's so sweet."

Game Five dawned quietly in town. Taro knew that he was going to be called upon to help lead the way in that game, and he was ready for the challenge. Now in his 11th season, Taro was a long-time veteran player in the NHL, and was ready to lead. He and Wayne were acknowledged as two of the team leaders, although Wayne actually wore the "C" as captain.

The game started with a bang, as Edmonton would score early, sending the fans into a frenzy. A Taro's teammate from Buffalo, who ironically was drafted by Buffalo the same year as Taro, would play in his 100th NHL playoff game.

This game wasn't even close, as Edmonton would hang eight goals on Philadelphia, clinching their second straight Stanley Cup Championship. Wayne Gretzky would go on to score a record 47 points in the playoffs, and earn the playoff MVP trophy for the very first time.

After the parade, the celebrations, the interviews, the television and radio programs had ended, Taro and Taylor took some time to look back at what had happened, and look ahead at what was to come. Taro was entering the final year of his 5-year extension with the club, and he was, again, concerned that he would be traded. Taro scheduled a meeting with management to discuss the contract situation. He wanted some assurances that he could negotiate a new deal to stay in Edmonton for many more years to come. He would turn thirty years old in the fall, but had been playing for eleven years. Based on his numbers so far, he certainly didn't seem to give any hint that he was slowing down at all. Unfortunately, money trouble had been dogging the team owner for awhile, and there was already talk of contract problems with several players. Most of it was rumors, but Taro knew as well as anyone that rumors often get started with a bit of truth. The meeting ended with management telling Taro "not to worry, he'd be treated fairly when it was time to discuss a contract extension." Taro was immediately worried. He didn't tell Taylor right away how things had gone, but it was clear soon enough that he was worried about what had gone down. Taylor recalls:

"I knew that Taro was going to talk about an extension with the team. I told him not to ask for too much,

or things would go badly right away. He knew what he was doing, at least that's what he told me.

When he came home, he didn't say much about the meeting. For a few days, he was distracted and not quite all together. After a week had gone by, I finally confronted him about it, and he told me that he'd been left hanging. I suggested that he play out his contract and then look elsewhere. He countered that by saying he'd be traded first, to make sure that the club got something worthwhile in return. With his numbers, and playoff experience, he was going to bring quite a return to Edmonton. That didn't exactly fill me with confidence. I liked living in Edmonton, and didn't want to move anywhere. I had grown up there, and loved the city very much. I was also fairly close to my parents.

If Taro was traded during the season, I figured I would probably stay here until the off-season, and see where he landed. If he could get a long-term deal, meaning at least three years, then we'd get a new house and settle in the city. If he only had a one-year deal, we would probably rent. It was all so daunting at that point."

Taro began to prepare himself for a possible trade. Nothing happened in the summer, and Taro made sure that he was in top shape, so as not to give any reason to trade him away. He got a very big confidence booster just before training camp, when none other than Wayne himself announced that he wanted the team to hang onto Taro. To the Japanese hockey player, it was just the sort of thing that you wanted to hear, especially heading into training camp.

Taro and his teammates would start the season flying, going 16 wins, 4 losses and 3 tie games by the end of November. Taro would score his 300th career goal early into the season, with, naturally, assists from Wayne and Mark. That assist by Wayne, interestingly enough, would be his 700th career assist.

They were on fire early in the year, and it showed in Taro's attitude. He was flying up and down the ice every shift of every game. In early December, Taro would, once again, show off his keen passing and on-ice vision. When Taro put up a stretch where he was notching more points than Wayne in every single game, the entire team joked that Taro was putting him out of business. Never mind that Wayne had almost more assists than Taro, he delighted in highlighting his teammates skills. Taro and Wayne were always joking about each other with the press, usually poking fun at themselves, while making the other out to be a much better player. Of course, for Taro, it was usually true that

Wayne was better.

As the new year rolled close, Taro would finish 1985 in style, as well as begin 1986 in equal style. Taro would set up two goals for Wayne, as he put up his 36th NHL hat trick. Two days later, Taro and yet another rookie player set each other up for a goal. The youngster would score his first Gordie Howe hat trick.

This is a hockey term for when a player scores a goal, an assist, and a fight in one game. It's named after the legendary Gordie Howe, who, ironically, did not have more than a handful of them in his illustrious 20+ year career. It's still associated with him, though. Hockey fans all over North America are familiar with the term. Taro wasn't familiar with the term until someone explained it to him after that game.

Taro had never been in a single fight to this point in his career. He still hoped to avoid them the rest of his career. He didn't see a point in risking injury by engaging in something that wasn't his job on the ice. The team knew this, and protected him. With plenty of muscle on the team, there was no need for Taro to engage in fighting.

As the trade deadline drew closer, Taro seemingly didn't care. He was too busy performing on the ice. He helped set up one teammate for his 50th goal on March 4th. Ten days later, he helped set up another player's 50th goal. Four days after that, on March 18th, he set up Wayne's 50th goal. It got to be a running joke that year, hearing the players referring to Taro as "Mr. Fifty" for awhile. Taro himself didn't care one bit; he actually enjoyed the attention and completely understood the joke.

As for the trade deadline, Taro stayed in Edmonton. If it was a big goal that season, chances are very good that Taro would have a hand in it. With his passing prowess, it's a wonder that Taro found time to score goals as well.

By the end of the season, Edmonton would win their 5th straight division title. Offensively, the team scored a total of at least 400 goals for the 5th straight year.

For Taro, he would put up 31 goals for the year, and also put up 110 points overall. This would be his 7th career 30+ goal season, as well as his fifth straight 100+ point season. As for career landmarks, Taro would pass 300 career goals, 600 career assists, and crack 900 total points.

But it was all going to come crashing down on them in the playoffs....

Chapter 6
1986 Playoffs

The first round would be a quick three-game sweep of the Vancouver. No big deal there. That was expected. That propelled them into a second round match up with none other than their Alberta rivals, Calgary.

Edmonton started having trouble with Calgary almost at once, when Calgary took Game One by a 4-1 score. For whatever reason, Taro and company never totally got back on track, and could never pull ahead in the series. They would go back and forth, Calgary taking a series lead, and Edmonton somehow managing to tie it back up. When Edmonton won Game Six in Calgary, they came home supremely confident. Everything looked great at that point. Taro arranged for Taylor's parents to come to Game Seven, and watch the Oilers finish off their pesky rivals. Naturally, Taylor's parents wore their Calgary jerseys, but still wore Taro buttons to cheer on their son-in-law. This created all sorts of weird looks, but it wasn't a big deal to them. Here in

Game Seven, it was a winner-take-all situation, and many fans didn't appreciate the Calgary jerseys. Fortunately, security kept an eye on them. But that would be the least of their worries.

It seemed, however, that fate had different plans in place for Taro and his teammates that night.

The game was tied at two apiece late in the 3rd period. Taro had scored one of Edmonton's goals, and was buzzing around looking for the go-ahead goal.

That's when fate, bad luck, or destiny turned on Edmonton.

One of the younger defensemen, a player named Steve, was playing the puck behind the Edmonton net, and went to make an outlet pass, to move the puck, and the team up the ice. Unfortunately, the puck would hit the goalie's skate, and bounce directly into the net, giving Calgary the lead. The arena, the fans, and the everyone in the packed arena all went silent in disbelief, watching the opposition celebrate. Despite their Calgary jerseys, Taylor's parents watched that goal in stunned silence as Calgary celebrated.

Edmonton wasn't able to come back, and had to watch Calgary win the game and the series. It also would end any chance Edmonton had of winning a 3rd straight Stanley Cup. It was a heartbreaking loss for everyone on the roster, and Taro was no different. Now, instead of playing on into late May, he was out of the playoffs by the end of April.

Taro went into self-imposed seclusion for three days, not leaving home at all. He blamed himself for the loss, saying that he hadn't scored enough goals in the series. Taylor was used to this sort of thing, as Taro had been known to get quiet and moody during the season if he had a bad game or two. Taro recalls:

> "It was a heartbreaking moment to see the series against Calgary decided on a missed opportunity. Everyone knows that Steve had never been intended for the puck to go anywhere near the goalie. What happened was a fluke, a freak moment in time. Calgary definitely was able to take advantage of the moment, and held us off for the rest of the game.
>
> Sure, I took it personally that I couldn't tie the game near the end. I should have been able to make something happen. After the game, and the season, had ended, well, I hid at home for three days. I helped out with everything I possibly could do at home, but I didn't go anywhere, and I didn't talk to anyone outside of Taylor or the kids. It was my way of showing that I wasn't happy with my own performance."

He would snap out of it fairly soon, and started to prepare for the upcoming season even before the Finals were over. Of course, there was still one little wrinkle. He wasn't under contract past the end of June.

The team knew that they would need to keep the core of their team intact if they would have a chance of returning to the Finals. The team would only offer a one-year extension, so he accepted. It wasn't much, but at least he would have a chance to return and play with his teammates for another season. Taylor recalls:

> "Taro worried so much about the contract talks. He was even more worried the day of the meeting. I told him to just relax, and let things happen. Whatever happened, he could count on my support. Things were going to work out somehow. There was no way that upper management were going to simply walk away from a player with seven 30+ goal seasons. I was confident they would give Taro a long-term deal, so he would be a centerpiece for many years to come.
>
> When he got home, he had a single year plus a hefty signing bonus. We'd put a fair piece of that bonus away for the future. Taro worried so much about his future. I would constantly try to reassure him that things were going to work out. I'm not sure if he be-

lieved me, but I had to try."

Taro got the surprise of a lifetime in early July when his long-time hockey friend Danny called him. Taro remembers:

"I got a phone call from my pal Danny. We had been teammates back when we both broke into the NHL with Buffalo. Apparently, he had been signed by Edmonton. That was wonderful news, and I immediately offered him the guest room at our place while he got himself on his feet in Edmonton."

With a two-time champion to help with training, Danny was practicing like never before. But it was slowly becoming obvious that he had lost a step or two over the years. Taro was flying up and down the ice at his normal speed, and found that he was having to constantly slow down to let Danny keep up. Privately, Taro wondered if his best friend was on his last legs. Taro recalls:

"It wasn't as much fun as I thought it would be. Seeing Danny have that much trouble on the ice in practice, I knew he was going to have problems when training camp opened. I doubted he would be able to keep up with the core of the our roster. I didn't want to be the one to tell him, though. I knew I was looking at the end of my friend's career. It was only a matter of time before Danny would hang it up. No doubt, it was going to be sooner than later. But, much like with a dying friend, Taylor and I would do everything we possibly could in order to help him out."

It would be a difficult beginning of the 1986-87 season. The team would stumble a bit out of the gate, winning just two of their first six road games. However, in a home game early in the season against Chicago, Taro scored twice, and assisted on two other goals. One of those goals that he set up would prove to be the last NHL goal scored by Danny. It was a bittersweet moment, for at the time, neither of the men knew what would soon be happening. Danny would get hurt early in the season, and miss a large amount of time. It would also be near the end of the line another of Taro's teammates from Buffalo, a player named Lee. He would be traded in March, returning to Buffalo to finish the season, at which point he would retire from pro hockey.

Taro found it interesting that he was still going strong after all these years. Lee, Danny and Taro had all started with Buffalo at the same time, and Taro was the only one who looked like he could go another few years. Taro recalls:

"I remember talking with Danny a few days after he was hurt in a game. He told me, in no uncertain words, that he was planning to retire at the end of the year. He just couldn't see himself hanging on any longer. It was a lot of fun to play alongside me one more time, but it was time to leave the game. I knew that he would find a job somewhere in the game, either as a coach, a scout or something else. A person with his skills would no doubt land on his feet.

As for Lee, we had been teammates a lot longer in Edmonton. But I could tell that he was slowing down as well. When he was traded, back to Buffalo, I knew that my own career might be slowing down. I had heard a lot of rumors that money was becoming a problem in Edmonton, and the owner was trying to save money any way he could. I decided that I was going to play out my contract, and see what I might be able to get as a free agent. No doubt, someone with my skill set would be able to find a spot as a first or second line forward easy enough."

It was somewhere around this time that Taro started talking with Taylor about life after playing hockey. That he was going to stay in the game at some level wasn't in doubt. He just didn't know where he would land. Perhaps he would just wait and see what options were available when he was finished playing. Maybe he would take a year off and have some time with his family. Kimberly and Wayne were just turning four years old, and the two younger boys were now two years old. It made for a somewhat chaotic home life, but Taro enjoyed every minute with the kids.

Early in the season, Taro achieved a milestone. He notched his 1,000th career NHL point. Fittingly, he scored it setting up a teammate for a goal. A few days later, Taylor and all the kids were at the game when the team had a special ceremony for Taro's milestone. Taylor recalls:

"Mom, Dad, and all the kids were with us that night. Taro knew that something was going to happen. He just had that look about him. I put the kids in their hockey shirts, and I wore my Taro jersey, the one he had given me all those years ago.

We were standing in the shadows in the Zamboni corner, waiting for our cue. Mom and Dad helped lead the kids out, and I led the way out onto the carpet which had been placed on the ice. All the Edmonton players were on the blue line, facing us. The announcer made a short speech, and team ownership, as well as

our team captain, Wayne, was there to give him a silver stick. That was awesome, but apparently there was something else that no one else knew about. Wayne had called a couple of people to be present for this milestone.

So, out walks Danny. Taro was visibly moved by this appearance. They embraced for a moment. Lee skated over to do the same, to both men. The so-called "Buffalo Connection" posed for a photo. Taro's first head coach from Buffalo, came out and said a few words. By now, Taro was almost to the point of tears. That's when Wayne, with the help of his teammates, revealed the biggest surprise. Apparently, Wayne had arrange for Taro to receive a new van for the family. So, Mom and Dad drove our van back home, I drove the new one home with Taro and the kids.

I've seen Taro visibly moved by things before, like the birth of the kids, but never to this extreme. By the way, the silver stick that was presented to him holds a place of honor in the bedroom. We've got pictures of the guys from Buffalo, as well as a whole host of other pictures, all surrounding the stick. It was quite a night. One that Taro and I will never forget."

Still, on the ice, Taro was playing as strong as ever. On December 10th, he set up two of Wayne's three goals that night. A week later, Wayne would put up his 9th four-goal game and sure enough, Taro had three assists on that night. He was showing no signs of slowing down to this point, that was for sure.

Taro would achieve another milestone on December 30th. In Vancouver, he would play his 1,000th career NHL game. For a late round draft pick, from another country, a player who was given no chance to even make the NHL, let alone last this long, it was a momentous occasion. So, the team held another celebration for Taro on January 11th. Hosting their arch-rivals, Calgary, Taylor and the kids would show up again to be present when the team made a big presentation for this milestone. Again, Danny and Lee would take part in the celebration. This time, the focus was on longevity and not production.

Ironically, seven days later, Edmonton traveled for a road game, where they would play in Buffalo. His former team would hold their own celebration of Taro's achievements, the 1,000 games and 1,000 points. It was a fitting return to where it all began when Taro was a lot younger. He found that he missed Buffalo, and the fans. Taro made a short speech for the Buffalo fans that night. He recalls part of that speech:

"Each time I return to Buffalo, I am treated to a

hero's welcome. They are some of the best fans in the league. I made a special point of thanking the 'French Connection' players, for helping me thrive and hone my skills in my early days. I mentioned the general manager by name that night as well. He drafted me, and I owe him my entire hockey career. Without his vision, I would never have made it to the NHL. But it is the fans that I love most. They have supported me every single time I appear in this building. The Sabres have a loyal following, and they appreciate greatness. Apparently, Taro Tsujimoto is also appreciated.

    The signs around the building, the ones that said 'Taro says...' were the best. I never get tired of seeing those everywhere around the league. If I could play another thirty years in the league, I would still never get tired of seeing those signs. Apparently, I am still one of the most popular players in Buffalo. Jerseys with my name are still popular to purchase by the fans.

    Would I consider a chance to return to Buffalo for the end of my career? I would think about it, sure. Would I actually go? I don't know. I've already won a couple of Stanley Cup rings, so I've pretty much achieved everything a player could want. Who wouldn't want a 7-time thirty goal scorer on their roster? Of course, the answer to that would be... everyone. We shall see what the future holds.

In any case, Taylor and I are going to be together in whatever happens down the road."

Taro would help set up Wayne on his 50th goal as the season progressed. It was quite a ride to the end of the year and into the playoffs. Anxious to avoid the mistakes of last year's 2nd round upset, Edmonton entered the playoffs focused beyond belief. Everyone on the roster knew what to do, and knew the goal. There was only one goal, and that was to get back to the Finals and win a third championship in four years.

Edmonton would lose Game One against Los Angeles, but it served as a wake-up call, and alerted "the beast." They would rebound nicely. Taro would set up three goals for a teammate, who put up his second four-goal playoff game of his career. Taro led the way to a score of 13-3. They would win four straight against L.A., followed by a four-game sweep of Winnipeg in the next round. The Conference Final was a five-game win over Detroit, and went on to the Finals, where they would meet the only other team that year to put up 100-points. It would be a seven-game war against Philadelphia, with Edmonton prevailing in Game Seven by a 3-1 score.

Taro would win his third Stanley Cup title in four years,

and was on top of the hockey world once more. His 13th season in the league had ended with the title. It was almost becoming old hat.

But questions started to surround him almost immediately. Money was the big question, as in how would the team's upper management be able to keep everyone on the roster. Would Taro be staying with the squad, or would he go elsewhere?

That question would be answered on draft day. Taro Tsujimoto found himself on the way to Buffalo, for two prospects and three draft picks. The long-popular forward was about to return home, back to where it all started for him.

Chapter 7
Going Home

In the summer of 1987, Taro found himself moving his family to the East Coast. He was going back to Buffalo, where his career started. He found a much different team when he arrived at training camp that fall. In the last four seasons, the team had not even qualified for the playoffs in two of them, and the other two had been first round exits.

Taro would sign a 2-year deal, and get himself to Buffalo right away for the announcement. He got his family settled into Buffalo quickly. Taylor managed to secure a position with the ticket office. She adjusted quickly, and was often seen helping run promotions at the games as well. It was very common for members of special groups to walk out, after a game, with hockey pucks signed by Taro, as well as other players. She also started the first official "Taro Fan Club" where fans could sign up, and would receive, in return, a special hockey puck and button, monthly newsletters, and special fan-club only contests. Special prizes were awarded every week to fans whose names were drawn from membership lists. She would wear a Taro jersey on game nights most of the time.

There was some young talent in training camp to be seen, and Taro was quick to recognize it. Taro would hit it off with the number one overall draft pick in 1987, a skilled forward named Pierre. The two players would pair well on the ice, and off as well.

Of course, the team wasn't as good as the team in Edmonton that Taro had been part of, and he knew that going into Buffalo. His goal was to help his new team reach the playoffs, and travel as deep as possible into the playoffs as well.

On the ice, Taro was having trouble maintaining his numbers from past seasons. He was keyed upon almost every shift, and opposing teams knew that he was a threat. With less talent to draw attacking players away from Taro, he was forced to take matters into his own hands a lot more often. While this would often result in goals, it also would result in a lot more missed opportunities. Taro was able to post another thirty one-goal season, but the assists were down somewhat. It would be his eighth consecutive 30+ goal season, and ninth overall, but his overall point total had dropped to 88 points.

For the first time in three years, Buffalo would make the playoffs. Unfortunately, even Taro's heroic performance wasn't enough to help them, as they lost a first-round series to Boston in six games. It was the earliest Taro had been eliminated from the playoffs in a very long time.

With a lot more time to have with his family this off-season, Taro took the entire family to visit his father, who had moved to Portland, Oregon. Hiro was an executive in charge of the United States offices of his former Japanese business. Portland, with its strong Japanese community, was a natural choice to set up shop. Hiro also had a 28% minority interest in the local junior hockey team. The team was part of the Western Hockey League, a development league where the players are working hard to get spotted and drafted by a professional team and work their way up to the pro ranks. The idea of working with teenagers and helping develop them was of particular interest to Taro. It offered at least a glimmer of interest to a post-NHL career.

Ironically, it was this very same league, back in 1974, that had offered a potential landing point for Taro when he was looking at his options in hockey in North America. While New Westminster, the team that was looking at him, was no longer in the league, the league itself was a strong presence in developing talent for pro hockey.

Taylor took a liking to the Portland area right away. She and Taro took the kids into town and walked around for a large part of a day, exploring the city. By the end of their visit, Taylor had a large amount of visitor's information about the city. She recalls:

> "I couldn't believe how laid back and green Portland was when we went into town. People were very nice, and I love the way that Portland is laid out. It seems like a wonderful place to live, and I started to work on Taro, to see if he would consider moving here.
>
> I figure he'd be able to work with the hockey team in some capacity, and I might be able to work with the ticket office in some way. When I mentioned the idea to him, Taro was very interested. I guess the city made an impact on him as well. He promised to talk with his father and see what could be done."

With the future being planned, Taro returned to Buffalo. He focused simply on making the second round of the playoffs this year. He announced this goal to the team in training camp, and it became a rally cry as the pre-season started.

1988-89 Season

The season started with a stutter, as the team was barely even in wins and losses by early November. It wasn't the time for things to go bad, but they certainly did. During what ended up being an overtime loss to Edmonton on November 13th, Taro was hit hard into the boards by a former teammate. Taro would hit the boards awkwardly and hurt his wrist. It would ultimately cost him twelve games, and would end his consecutive games played streak at 1,141 games in a row. Mark would send a get-well card to Taro, apologizing for injuring his wrist. Taro sent his own card, saying that it was all in the line of duty, and not to worry too much about it.

While on the injured list, Taro would be able to celebrate birthdays for all the kids. It was the first time he had some time off during any season since he started in the NHL. While Taylor was working at the ticket office and with the Taro Fan Club, he stayed at home the first few games with the kids. When he was able, he would start practicing with the team. His wrist was healing nicely, and he bounced back quickly.

However, Taro found that he was enjoying being away from the game. He liked being with the kids and playing games with them. Kimberly and Wayne, now six years old, were in full-day kindergarten, and enjoying it. They were in an advanced reading group, and were far ahead of the rest of their class with math as well. Steve and Danny were four years old, and in full-day preschool. All three boys were in weekend ice hockey leagues as well. They were doing quite well, having practiced skating at a very early age, and Kimberly was skating regularly with the kids when they'd go out for fun at a nearby ice rink. At home, the three boys would shoot rolled-up socks at Kimberly. She was rapidly developing cat-like reflexes. Taro was beginning to think that his playing days would be coming to an end sooner than expected. He recalls:

> "I think Taylor was right about one thing. I did a lot of thinking while I was recovering at home. For the first time, I really let myself relax and enjoy being home with the kids. I would drive them to school, and have the day off. Sometimes, I would sit and watch movies. Other days, I would go meet Taylor at work in the ticket office, and help her with the fan club. I tried to go have lunch with the kids at least once a week at school.
>
> I heard from my father also. He said that I would be welcome to join the hockey team in Portland if I desired. They wouldn't elaborate, saying it was inappropriate to do so while I was still employed with Buffalo.

I promised to give the suggestion full consideration, and would also fly out to Portland for a more formal interview when my season was over. I mentioned it to Taylor, and she loved the idea."

He would make his long-awaited return on December 15th, and help guide the team to a 2-2 tie with Minnesota. The fans cheered for him every time he touched the puck. It was a successful return to action. Things were going smoothly for Taro, and he was in fine form as the season progressed.

...and that's about the time things took a nasty turn south...

One Bloody Night

Taylor and the rest of Taro's family were at the Buffalo-St. Louis game on March 22nd, 1989. All the kids were wearing their respective hockey gear; shirts, hats, even kid-sized sweats for Steve and Danny. They were a very cute pair of four-year old kids. Taylor had drawn three names from the Taro Fan Club list before the game, and they would receive prizes during the course of the game.

Tonight was a showdown with St. Louis, and the 74th game of the year for Buffalo. It was a pleasant evening as the teams took the ice to start the game. In goal for Buffalo was one of their young, promising goalies, a player named Clint.

Things looked pretty good for both teams as the game wore on, with each team scoring one goal in the early stages. Several times during the game, players would crash the goal, trying to create chaos and tip a shot into the net behind the goalie. It happens probably a hundred times every night in the NHL, and nothing seemed to be any different.

When the St. Louis player took the puck and headed in on goal, toward Clint, no one gave it much thought, other than to wonder if Buffalo's goalie would stop this shot the way he'd stopped many others.

What happened next, however, would end up being one

of the most horrific sights ever seen in the NHL.

The collision knocked Clint off his feet, during which time the St. Louis player's skate blade sliced through Clint's jugular vein, causing him to bleed profusely all over the ice. Clint ripped his helmet off, and medical staff ran to assist, pandemonium reigned. Later, reports from various media and team outlets would state that eleven fans watching the game fainted, two others had heart attacks, and three players vomited on the ice. While history does not recall the lucky, or unlucky, three players, Taro did recall the following:

> "I had just come onto the ice from a shift change when the collision happened. All I saw was blood all over the place, so I yelled for help. Other players started making similar calls, and I saw medical staff heading toward Clint. The entire arena went silent as the medics rushed to the goalmouth. Our trainer, a former Vietnam war veteran, gets credit for not only making it to the front of the goal in record time, but he definitely saved Clint's life with his quick thinking.
>
> I remember hearing someone off to one side of me making some extremely unpleasant sounds, but I didn't look. I didn't have to. I recognized those sounds, and I knew what was going on. To be honest, I barely

kept my lunch down as it was. I heard later that Clint needed three hundred stitches to close the wound. Unfortunately, they weren't able to clean the ice, and the rest of the game was played with a huge red splotch in front of that one goal.

After the game was over, over half the team went to the hospital to go visit him. I was out for a big piece of the night with my teammates, to check on Clint.

I saw Taylor for a short time after the game. All the kids hugged me tightly. Taylor gave me a huge hug as well, plus a few kisses of what had to be relief, I'm sure. She was just happy that I was in one piece. It certainly made me re-think my priorities on and off the ice. I think that's what finally pushed my mind to a decision."

Taylor recalls the incident from a different angle, up in the seats:

"I saw the collision in front of the goalie, and my first thought was to worry about a possible concussion. I started to worry that he might have been hit in the head. The collision was pretty intense. When I saw the growing puddle of blood, I made the kids all turn away, and hide their eyes. No need for them to see anything more than necessary. The entire building, filled with rowdy hockey fans, had gone completely silent. It was a little unnerving. I heard players yelling for help, saw the medics rushing from open doors to the front of the net. I watched Taro for a moment, just to make sure that he was all right, and he seemed to be moving all right. I think he was a little sick to his stomach, because he made a point of returning to the bench for what seemed like a lot of water. But at least he was moving on his own power. None of the other players on either team seemed hurt at that time.

I can't even imagine how that St. Louis player was feeling at that point. I have no idea what happened to him as things settled down. I would imagine he was completely shaken up. To his credit, he stayed in the game, however.

After Clint was helped off the ice and I could see Taro skating around on his own power, I let the kids look back at the ice. I had all the kids look down there at their dad, just so they would know that he was safe. It was the most gruesome thing I had ever seen or heard of in hockey. I found out from Taro a couple days later that Clint needed a couple hundred stitches to close the wound. I also found, again from Taro, that the trainer had used his Vietnam experience to save Clint's life

I vowed that night to have a very long discussion with Taro about his playing career, and whether or not he was going to keep playing. He told me, after the game, that he was going with much of the team to go visit Clint at the hospital. I wasn't going to stand in the way of that. Taro is a very caring person, and it didn't surprise me one bit that he was going to visit his teammate in the hospital.

I wasn't mad at him, I was scared for him. For the first time, I had seen a life-threatening injury, on the ice, in a game. The last thing I wanted was for something like this to happen to Taro.

Funny thing about something like this, it hit both of us equally hard. When Taro finally got home, he said he was rethinking how long he was going to keep playing. I think we both got the living daylights scared out of us. I certainly didn't want Taro to get seriously hurt playing hockey. We have a family and I want him to be able to play with the kids and spend time with them in the future as well."

Clint was present at a press conference a couple days later, and joked with reporters about "having a new place to hold a pen or two." He was remarkably upbeat, considering he had come within an inch or so of losing his life. Less than two weeks later, Clint would return to the arena where he almost lost his life.

Taylor would spend parts of the next several days fielding phone calls from friends all over the hockey world. Two questions were on their minds. First, was Taro all right? Second? How bad was Clint injured, and how was his recovery going? She reassured everyone that Taro was just fine, and that Clint seemed to be doing well. Taro called his father and they spoke for nearly thirty minutes. Taylor recalls that it seemed like a one-sided conversation, and Taro spent a lot of the time listening.

It was apparent that Taro was suddenly having second thoughts about the length of his career. He was in the process of finishing up his fifteenth season. Perhaps it was time to consider options such as retirement already. His father was already trying to line up a post-playing career position for Taro at the junior level. Taro recalls that thought process:

> "After watching Clint get his neck cut on the ice, I think I started to consider retirement much more seriously. I didn't want anything serious to happen to me in the game. I owed it to Taylor and all the kids to

think of them when it came to my safety.

I had already missed twelve games during that year, and found that I enjoyed being away from the game. I had been concerned about how I would handle the time away from the ice, but it wasn't nearly as tough as I thought it would be. It was time well spent, being with the kids, teaching them to play hockey, having lunch with them during the day, or taking them out and about. Retirement was something that I was willing to consider at this point. Taylor and I spent the rest of the regular season discussing it. I finally decided, after the last game of the season, that I was going to announce my retirement more or less at the end of the playoff run. It wasn't going to be easy, but it was time to do it.

Funny thing about that decision. Once I made up my mind, and called my father, I found that a huge weight was off my shoulders. I was a lot happier at home and at the ice rink. I still didn't say anything to anyone on the team, so news wouldn't get out until I chose to make my announcement."

Taro would score his 400th career goal during the season. It certainly would have come sooner, except for the injury.

He would also post his 1,200th career point. The playoff run was short, a five game series loss to Boston in the first round, and by mid-April, Taro and the team were done for the year.

Shortly after the playoffs ended, Taro requested, and was granted, a meeting with upper management. In that meeting, he stated that he was planning to retire, effective immediately. There was, of course, plenty of disbelief and confusion on the part of team staff. Taro recalls:

"It wasn't an easy choice for them to hear. But I made it clear that I was finished playing in the NHL. The team made the official announcement. I was heart-broken, but I stated that it was my time to hang it up before I became a shadow of my former self. My goals scored for this past season was the lowest total in nine years. It was time to leave the game. I wanted to leave professional hockey before it was clear that I had held on too long. I didn't want people to think that Taro, former star player, should have retired a year or two earlier.

Taylor, as I remember, was somewhat disappointed because the Taro Fan Club was coming to an end. On the other hand, not playing meant that the risk of skate cuts dropped to nearly zero."

The Legend of Taro Tsujimoto

Now, he would be free to go to Portland, and join his father with the junior team. It would be a new challenge, one that Taro was eagerly looking forward to accepting.

Chapter 8

Over the summer, Taro and the family took another vacation to Portland, Oregon. Taylor was in love with the city, and wanted to move there eventually. Taro would end up purchasing eight percent of the junior hockey team from his father. This vacation would soon become a house hunting trip, and the Tsujimoto family would soon head west, to Portland.

Taro got his family settled in Portland quickly. Taylor found work right away with the Winterhawks ticket office. She had plenty of experience and was the right person at the right time. It would be a perfect fit. She also was invited to spend one day a week, at first, working with the team's General Manager. Apparently, the GM wanted her to start learning the ropes right away.

The kids all started school in the fall, and would quickly adjust to the new city. All three of the boys would start playing hockey in the fall as well, As the older of the three boys, Wayne was alone in a league, while Steve and Danny would join a team at their age level. Kimberly had proved to be quite adept at stopping pucks, so Taro encouraged her to get into goalie school. Taylor recalls:

> "When Kimberly showed that she was able to stop a lot of the shots the boys were taking, Taro decided that she could at least try out to be a goalie. I wasn't so sure, but I knew she would get a lot of practice with three boys at home.
>
> Turns out that Kim was very good, and she had game. So, Taro and I enrolled her in the same level as Wayne. It was tough to get a team to accept her, at least until she demonstrated her skills. At that point, three teams started jockeying for her services. Kimberly ended up playing as a backup goalie on Wayne's team. Turns out Wayne liked the idea of his twin sister on his team."

Taro was free to start working with Portland right away. Taro started out scouting some players in nearby towns for the summer. He would work with the players in rookie camp, and then move on to training camp as well. Portland wanted him to help develop some of their younger players and help them get ready for the upcoming season.

He was going to be an assistant coach in the junior ranks, helping develop talent to prepare them for the NHL. Portland was coming off a trip to the WHL Finals, where they had been swept. Taro had his work cut out for him. He was going to inherit a team that was losing a lot of their stars.

To say that the 1989-90 season was bad was an understatement. It was not the way that Taro wanted to start out his second career. Learning to work with young players who were between ages sixteen and twenty was a new concept for Taro, but one that he was adjusting to fairly well. While he was having trouble in his first season as a coach, it was widely acknowledged that he did well with the talent that was on the roster. That was about all that Taro could ask for at this point. He recalls:

> "Talk about a difference in coaching style. I was used to dealing with people who, in most cases, had played a number of years in the league and pretty much had their act together. Now, as an assistant, he had to help kids who may or may not be able to adjust to this level of hockey. Making the leap to major junior, where Portland was at, was a significant jump in many respects. These players had to learn to live away from

home. In some cases, these players could be thousands of miles away. Some of the guys had to mature faster than others, and, well, in my mind, some of the guys on the roster that year just weren't ready to play in the WHL.

I had to learn quickly how to relate to teenagers. Fortunately, with a little help from Taylor, I was able to learn and adjust. Patience became my friend."

Clearly, Taro had a rough first year. He was starting to find a style of coaching that would work for him around the time that the season ended. No worries, the team was committed to him for the long term. They liked having an NHL player on the coaching staff, and gave him a vote of confidence at the end of the year.

With Portland's season over by mid-March, Taro was able to spend more time at home. Of course, he was still doing some scouting work in the spring, watching players in their respective playoff seasons. It helped pass the time as March slowly passed into April.

In his time off, Taro was watching his kids play hockey. He had declined an offer to coach his kids team, because he didn't want to influence them, and because he was working so much as it was. It was going to be up to them to decide how to play, and how to learn from the existing coaching staff.

Wayne was especially good at his level, and proved to have plenty of skill. Some people wondered if he had inherited Taro's abilities. For a seven-year old, Wayne was quite a hockey player. Kimberly was proving to be a good goalie. The other two boys, Steve and Danny, were on the same team and were even linemates. They would race up and down the ice together, passing back and forth until one of them would shoot the puck, and if he missed, the other was usually there for the rebound. Of course, the term "race up and down the ice" is relative for five-year old kids.

Taro watched the kids whenever he was at home, which was often. Taylor became the proto-typical "hockey mom." Armed with a rather sizable van, she would help drive players around town to games, at least when she wasn't busy in the ticket office, or working with the General Manager's staff.

At the end of their seasons, all the kids were having parties to celebrate. Wayne and Kim's team would win their league title, and they celebrated by asking Taro to skate around the rink with him and the trophy. Taro recalls:

"Wayne and Kim both asked me to bring my skates to the final game. They said that if their team won, they both wanted me to skate with him around the rink.

Wayne wanted me to put on an NHL jersey and skate like I'd won the Stanley Cup. Sure enough, they won the game. After the other team had left the ice, and things had settled down a little bit, I went on the ice with the team and skated around with them. Kimberly and Wayne were leading the charge around the rink. It's a lot of fun to skate with a herd of seven-year olds who want nothing more than to play the game and have fun at it. Steve and Danny were playing the following day, but since this was more like a party, I called on them to come on the ice and celebrate with their brother. I took pictures of them together, and they've got framed photos on their bedrooms walls.

I'm very proud of Wayne. He never once told his younger brothers to go away or to get lost. He wanted to celebrate with them, and share the party. It was a very grown-up move. I guess I've raised them well so far."

A few days later, Steve and Danny would celebrate with their team, as they led the way to a league title of their own. This time, Steve and Danny would return the favor and celebrate with their older brother and Kim. It was a lot of fun for the entire family as the days and months went by in the spring. Everyone was doing quite well in their first year in Portland.

Taro was instrumental in bringing a couple of potential stars to Portland for the 91-92 season. It would seem that the "Legend of Taro" was already starting to take effect in Portland. Players liked the idea of learning from a long-time NHL veteran with three Stanley Cup rings. The team was starting to gel, and things came together rather well. At least they made the playoffs this season, the first time since Taro had become an assistant coach. He still wasn't happy with his performance, but at least he was learning to be a better coach.

Portland would get bounced in the first-round of the playoffs, losing in six games to Spokane. That left Taro out of action by the beginning of April. Again, he was able to spend a lot of the spring with his family, when he wasn't off scouting players. Taylor had been promoted to senior account manager in the ticket office. She had done extremely well in her short time with the team. She proudly displayed pictures of the family at her desk; pictures of her and Taro with famous NHL players such as Gretzky. Taylor also had built up a collection of NHL jerseys, and proudly showed them off at the ticket office, or on game nights. She would sometimes wear her Taro jersey from Edmonton. Other days, it would be a Buffalo jersey. All in all, it was a great start to living in Portland.

Watching all of the kids play hockey was a fun way to

relax for Taro and Taylor. Wayne was turning out to be quite a player for a nine-year old. Steve and Danny were not far behind as seven-year olds, and although she had a late start playing goalie, Kimberly was turning into a rather skilled netminder. All the kids were bringing home awards and trophies on a regular basis, and the family had to find space for all the awards. Taro and the boys would end up building large shelves for everything.

As the summer wore on, Taro would help bring in a couple of highly-rated prospects. Both of these players would make the Portland roster as sixteen-year olds, and would soon become impact players. Taro was extremely pleased with these players, and team management was pleased with Taro's scouting eye.

Taro would be honored by the Hockey Hall of Fame on his first year of eligibility. He was voted to join the hallowed halls of Hockey as the first Japanese player to be elected. While the kids would stay for a week with Taylor's parents, Taro and Taylor would fly to Toronto for the induction ceremonies. Taro recalls the entire trip:

> **"I never thought I would play long enough, or be good enough to even be considered for the Hall of Fame. My teammates in Edmonton, as well as Buffalo, sent waves of letters congratulating me on my newest honor. I had a tough time speaking when my turn**

came around, but somehow, with a little encouragement from Taylor, who was sitting in the front row, I managed to get my speech out. People asked which uniform I should be pictured in and I wanted to wear Buffalo's colors, but ultimately, it was decided that my Edmonton career would be more appropriate since that's where my biggest success happened."

Taylor recalls things pretty much the same way:

"Taro was the last person to actually accept that he was a member of the Hall of Fame, even after the official announcement had arrived. He never thought, for a minute, that he was that good. I knew it all along. I wasn't nearly as surprised to hear the news, although, personally, I wasn't sure he would make it on the first try. Mom and Dad kept the kids for a week while we flew to Toronto for the ceremonies. I wore one of his Edmonton jerseys and had a chance to buy some other jerseys while I was there. Hey, let's have some fun shopping while on the road, right? Anyway, honoring Taro was a lot of fun. Now, he's going to be remembered forever in hockey's biggest stage. He and I also have lifetime memberships now, so we can go anytime we want. That's going to be fun. I even heard that they want to put some of his Japanese hockey stuff on display too. An entire viewing case of Taro's stuff, that's the last thing he ever expected. I'm so proud of him."

1992-93 Portland Season

Portland would improve on the previous season, winning 14 more games this season. Taro spent a lot of time either on the road, or behind the scenes during much of the year. At one point, he spent a weekend in Seattle scouting for a potential trade. When it happened, the results were even better than expected. One player in particular, acquired from Seattle, would end up scoring more than a point per game, 37 points in just 27 games with Portland during the regular season. Certainly, Taro had an eye for talent, and everyone behind the scenes was beginning to appreciate Taro's vision. He was definitely building for both the present, and the future. Taro recalls:

"I have been asked how I recognized this guy's talent in Seattle. I knew that by watching his initial movements around the net, as well as his acceleration, he would be an excellent fit. Of course, no one expected him to win the scoring title the following year with Portland. But it sure made me look like a genius. Every so often a person finds a diamond in the rough, or a player that just needs a change of scenery. This guy did, and it worked."

As Portland headed into the playoffs, everything looked promising. Portland won the division by three points, and was in a position to potentially challenge for the entire league title. That's what Taro thought as the playoffs began.

Portland started the playoffs strong, with a first round sweep. It was a very convincing performance, but at the same time, it was a performance that was expected. Finishing forty-three points ahead of the other team does that sort of thing to a team's expectations. Things didn't let up as they marched and destroyed everyone in their path in the Western Conference.

Ultimately, Portland would clinch the Western Conference title, and advance to the League Championship, where they would meet Swift Current. In a hard-fought battle, the two teams would go the distance, with Portland eventually losing in Game Seven.

Disappointment was evident as the team returned to Portland. But for Taro, things were about to get much worse.

He would be home for barely 24 hours before receiving a telephone call from Japan. His father, Hiro, had gone back to Tokyo to spend about a month for business. Now, it seemed, Hiro was very ill and in a hospital. Taro immediately flew to Tokyo to see his father. Taro recalls:

"I remember getting home in the middle of the

night from Swift Current. It was a disappointing way to end the season, but I knew that we had played our very best hockey. We simply ran up against a stronger club that was able to step up their game when it mattered most.

I wasn't home more than a few hours when Taylor woke me. My father, Hiro, was in the hospital and wanted to see me. He used the phrase 'before it's too late,' which really scared me. I had never heard those words from him before, and I didn't know what to make of it. I quickly packed a suitcase and left Taylor with the kids for a few days.

Upon arrival, I went straight to the hospital, not even going to the hotel first. He didn't look very good. He was pale and withdrawn. I sat with him for nearly a day before he finally woke up enough to converse with me. He was also going to transfer his accounts to my name. What did this mean to my family and I? Simply put, he was selling his share of the hockey team, as well as putting all of his assets in my name. I was going to receive it all within the next thirty days, by way of his law assistants. While I was very excited, I was also humbled by this gesture.

I found out later that evening, from the doctor,

that my father wasn't going to make it another couple of days. He was just too sick."

Taro called Taylor right away, forgetting the time zone differences. She recalls:

"Taro called very early in the morning, and I knew something was wrong. The last thing he would have done would be to wake me at that hour unless he didn't know or had forgotten about the time zone change. He told me what was going on, and that his father wasn't going to make it. I reminded him that he had to be strong, for his family name. We would grieve at home, later on.

I knew the kids were going to miss him, but I wasn't going to make a big deal out of it just yet. I wasn't even sure how to tell them yet, since they were all relatively young. Kimberly and Wayne were eleven, and Steve and Danny were nine. It can be a challenge to tell kids at these ages about death in the family.

I just asked Taro to take it easy, and I would meet him at the airport when he returned."

As expected, Hiro Tsujimoto passed away about twenty-seven hours after Taro arrived at the hospital. Taro arranged for the body to be cremated. The house in Tokyo was to be dealt with by a family member, but Taro was able to ship several boxes of items that had been his at one point to Portland. Things that had been his as a kid, growing up in Tokyo. Hiro had saved several hockey mementos from Taro's youth, and those would be sent to Portland. It was a very somber occasion, punctuated with several glasses of sake and a great deal of remembrance and introspection as well.

A memorial service was held in Portland as well, where many of Hiro's business clients, as well as members of the Portland team office, would put in appearances and pay their last respects.

The team approved the transfer of ownership of Hiro's share of the team to Taro almost immediately. The Western Hockey League would do the same within a month.

Taro threw everything that he had into scouting and preparing for the upcoming season. He rarely spoke about his loss at home, or with anyone for that matter. Taylor recalls:

> "After the memorials, the trip to Tokyo, and the final arrangements for his father, Taro was very withdrawn at home. He wasn't going to watch the kids play hockey. He didn't do much at home except stay in the

office, working on stuff for the team. I was very worried about him for days.

I finally forced the issue in early June, about the time that the kids were finishing the school year. I told him, basically, that it was time to wake up and re-join the family. He was surprised by my forcefulness, but I think he saw the error of his ways. It was about a week after school was out that he took everyone to the coast for a few days. It was a fun vacation, and a chance for us to get back together. Hey, I worry about him a lot, but it doesn't mean that he can mope around and ignore those closest to him."

Thanks to timely intervention from Taylor, he was able to pull himself back out of the blue. Taro would take the family to the Oregon Coast for a week. They spent time at the aquarium in Newport, walking amongst the fish and other aquatic creatures. They walked on the beach, picking up a rather impressive collection of seashells and rocks. Taylor showed the kids a few ways to fly kites, while Taro showed them one very important way not to do the same. The kids learned pretty fast, while Taro just couldn't seem to keep his kite in the air. It provided several laughs for the entire family, and helped lighten Taro's mood. Later in the evening, after the kids had gone to bed, Taro admitted to Taylor that he had been deliberately crashing his kite just to make everyone laugh.

Another day, Taro took everyone further south near Florence, to the Sea Lion Caves. After buying the tickets, they all went to the elevator, and rode it down to the caves underground. Sea lions swim in and out from the ocean, and this was a safe place, set back some distance, where the animals could stay sheltered from the ocean. It was a fun day trip, and the kids enjoyed it immensely. On the way back to their motel, they stopped in Depoe Bay and stood by the seawall. At high tide, the waves slam into the rocks, sending a huge shower of water up into the air, drenching passersby. The kids thought it was fun, although Taylor stayed back a short distance to avoid getting wet. Everyone would pick up a small supply of salt water taffy. Some of the best on the entire coastline was available in Depoe Bay. Side note; Depoe Bay has the world's smallest harbor. Wayne thought that fact was rather interesting, as did Kimberly.

As the week-long adventure came to a close, Taro and Taylor felt that the primary goal had been accomplished. The family had come back together, and Taro had managed to re-center himself. On the last day, after they had checked out of the motel, Taro drove the family down to the beach one final time.

This time, however, he asked that the family remain at the car. Taylor recalls:

"I held the kids back, allowing him to go down to the beach alone. He was down there for several minutes by himself. At one point, he kneeled in the sand, and bowed in the direction of the ocean. I gathered that he was saying a prayer of some sort for his father. He was facing west, toward Japan. I quietly asked the kids not to say anything about what had transpired. If Taro was going to tell us what was going on, he would say it in his own time.

When he returned, he didn't say anything, other than to ask if we were ready to head home. We were ready, and so we left the beach. He told me later that night that he was, indeed, saying a prayer to Hiro, and that the beach had provided the proper moment for such circumstances."

Taro recalls the moment his own way:

"I didn't say anything to anyone, but I think Taylor knew what was going on. I walked down to the beach and kneeled in the sand. I bowed to the west, facing my homeland, Japan. I spent several minutes saying prayers to my father, encouraging him to move on to the next challenge for his spirit. I asked for his forgiveness, because we didn't have a chance to connect the way that we should have in the past. I closed by wishing him the very best on his journey to the beyond, and asked that he help me regain my path to success. I had fallen off that path in the last few months, and needed to re-center myself. I thanked his spirit one final time, and headed back to the car.

I think Taylor had asked the kids not to say anything, because I could see the questions on their faces. But no one ever asked me about it on the ride home. Taylor confirmed that to me in the evening. She wrapped her arms around me and held me for quite some time, in the dark room. It was a fitting end to the day."

As the summer came slowly to an end, the hockey season started with a vengeance. Taro was determined to help lead the way to the league title again, and improve the only way a team can after losing Game 7 in the league finals.

Over the next four years, Taro and the family had a great deal of personal successes. Taylor was moving beyond just ticket sales, and had become an executive assistant to the General Manager. She was doing a lot of the office work for the GM, and was gaining an insiders look at the position. Rumor had it that she was potentially being groomed to move into the position in a few years if she continued growing at this pace.

Wayne Tsujimoto would be drafted by Spokane in the third round of the 1997 WHL Bantam Draft. The Bantam Draft is where all the clubs draft fifteen year-old players from eligible locations in North America. The players then become the property of the WHL clubs and challenge for the right to play in the league. Taro was pleased to hear that his oldest son had been drafted into the league. Three days later, surprise rocked the league when it was announced, that Kimberly Tsujimoto had been signed as a free agent by Seattle. She was the first female player to be signed by a WHL club. Taylor and Taro had been alerted ahead of time, so they could be present in Seattle at the team offices in Seattle when she officially signed her education contract.

Players in the WHL sign contracts that are good for one year of Canadian college for each year that they play in the league. It also means that the player gives up any and all ability to play in the United States NCAA college hockey system. Taro and Taylor would take the family to Spokane for a couple of days, and watch Wayne sign his contract. It was an emotional moment for the family as the oldest kids took their next steps in hockey. They stopped in Seattle on the way home, and Kimberly signed her contract at that time. Both of them would return home with hats from their respective clubs.

Taylor recalls:

"I know that Wayne took it for granted that he would be drafted by some team in the WHL. Still, to be drafted in the third round, he was surprised. I knew that he was going to make it, simply on sheer determination and grit. That's the sort of player that he had developed into.

As for Kimberly, she was a long shot. But the fact that she had signed an education contract was an important step. Seattle evidently thought that she had potential, and was willing to take a chance on her. I know that she was worried about making it on her own merits, and not just based on the fact that her father was an NHL star. Of course, she was a goalie, and not a skater. That meant she had to make it or not without any help from dear old dad. It's what she wanted, however. Kimberly wanted to make it on her own ability, not on name alone.

Taro and I were pleased as can be about seeing them both signing with WHL clubs. They would still be spending one more year in Portland, with their current teams. Fifteen year old players can only play a total of five games before the end of their current team's season. I would be able to watch them play for one more year."

Taro has similar recollections:

"It was an honor to see Wayne drafted in the league. I knew he would work hard and have an excellent chance at making the Spokane roster soon enough. I wasn't so sure if Kimberly would make it, but I knew that she had the potential to challenge for a position in the league soon enough. That was enough for her.

I worked with both Wayne and Kimberly during the off-season. I would take a lot of shots at Kimberly, which she told me later would help her improve her skills. Wayne and I would rapid-fire a lot of shots as well. Both of them benefited from my help over the summer. But at the same time, I told them that they had to make it on their own when they started the season in the fall. I could only do so much to help, and I really didn't want to affect their games at this point in their careers."

The stage was set for the 1997-98 season. Over the summer, Taylor was named Assistant General Manger, the first woman to achieve that position in the WHL. It was a sign that she had broken through the so-called glass ceiling, and was making strides never before seen at this level. Of course, it meant that she was going to be even more busy than ever before, but it was a challenge that she would meet head on, eagerly to be sure. With the kids all off either at school in town or off playing hockey in other areas, she wasn't as tied down as she had been in previous years.

Rumors abounded that Taro was in a position to move up to take a head coaching position in the near future, but he refused to speak to that subject. He recalls:

> "I know that many people were talking about me possibly taking over the Portland head coaching position in the next few years. It was equally possible that I could be going elsewhere in the league as a head coach. I took it all with a grain of salt. If that's what was going to happen, then so be it. I liked being in Portland. Taylor and I both liked it here. I didn't want to leave, but if the right position came along, then I was willing to listen.
>
> At the moment, however, we had bigger fish to fry.

The season was about to start, and things looked good from the get-go."

Looked good? That's putting it mildly. As the season progressed, it became clear that Portland was a force to be reckoned with, and they were nearly unstoppable. Portland would never lose two consecutive games during the entire season. Oh sure, they had a stretch where they did not win three games in a row, but that was a loss, a tie, and another loss. On the flip side, the team did roll up a fifteen game winning streak. One of the forwards that Taro had scouted was showing some incredible offense that season. He would put up 109 points to lead the team. He was quite a playmaker, something that Taro says was a natural ability, but others say that Taro may have helped develop to some degree.

In any case, Portland had really come together this season, and it showed in their on-ice performance. The team was flying up and down the rink every night. Taro was busy with the power play units during each game, but he found that it was pretty easy to keep track of things. The players knew their responsibilities, and they took care of business. Taro would later call it his easiest season yet.

On another note, Spokane would call up Wayne just after Christmas, and he would play in two home games. Weather prevented Taylor and the rest of the family from watching his first game in the league in person. However, Wayne called home after the game to tell everyone that he had scored his first WHL goal. He was on cloud nine, and rightfully so.

Moments like those were most definitely going to be more common as Wayne's season progressed. Wayne would be sent back to Portland to finish out the season with his Bantam level team. But he had proven that he belonged in the WHL, and that was a very important step for a player his age. He was on his way. Taro was proud of his oldest son, and of Kimberly as well. She was putting up numbers that were rather impressive.

In the middle of a long stretch of home games, Taro and Taylor were sometimes able to go watch Wayne's team in action while he played in Portland. Anytime that Taro and Taylor were out at a hockey game, there was always an eye out for new talent, and this was no exception. But for the most part, it was a chance to watch their oldest son play hockey and enjoy it.

For this game, Wayne's team was playing against Kimberly's team. This happened a total of eight times during the season. Taro and Taylor would meet with the kids for a few minutes before the game, but otherwise left them alone.

Kimberly started in goal for her team. So far on the season, she had a 2.41 goals against average. This meant that for the season, she averaged that many goals scored against her per game. She also had a save percentage of 92.7%. Put simply, that percentage represented the number of shots stopped per one hundred shots faced.

During the first period, Taro had several grade-school age kids come up to him, asking if they could get pictures with him or if he would sign hats for them. "Occupational hazard" is what Taro called it. He didn't mind the attention for the most part. Occasionally, Taro would ask for an usher to hold back the throngs of autograph hounds, but for the most part, he let things take a natural course. Taylor, of course, was used to it by now, being married to a hockey star for years.

That night's game was a physical affair, with both teams throwing body checks left and right. Wayne was flying back and forth across the ice rink. Apparently, he had inherited some speed from his father. Kimberly, on the other hand, was a smaller goalie with cat-like reflexes. She could, and did, almost leap from one side to the other of the goal and block shots that most goalies would have trouble stopping.

On one power play in the second period, Wayne was standing in front of the goal, right in front of his sister. Wayne saw the shot coming, and turned to look for a rebound. He got blasted in the back by a defender, and slammed into Kimberly, knocking both of them down to the ice. Somehow, she stopped the puck, but there was a big pile of bodies. Most times, things would have stopped there with a lot of words and maybe some pushing and shoving. But as Wayne stood up, he asked Kimberly if she was all right. That's when one of her teammates hauled off and sucker-punched Wayne in the face. He promptly dropped onto the ice while chaos reigned. The officials managed to get things under control, but only after nearly fifteen minutes had elapsed.

When it was all said and done, and a lot more was done than said, three players on both sides were thrown out of the game and one more on each side would spend time in the penalty box. Ironically, both Kimberly and Wayne somehow managed to avoid being penalized. Wayne remembers it this way:

"I know that I was standing in front of the net, looking for a rebound. I've got great hand-eye coordination so I spend a lot of time in front of the net. Somehow, I suspect that if I hadn't checked on Kimberly, I wouldn't have been sucker-punched. But she's my sister, and I fell over her. She was fine, and gave me a firm shove. It was all in the moment of the game, so I wasn't too worried about it. But I think that guy that hit me thought I was trash-talking her. So he hit me. It was probably a good thing that he got thrown out, because I would have gone back to even the score."

Wayne re-learned a valuable lesson after that. Just because your sibling is on the ice, you don't talk to them during the game. Many players do at least make a cursory check on the opposing player if they get hit like that. But it's just enough to make sure people are not hurt.

In any case, the game ended without anything else nasty breaking out. Wayne would get three goals, and Kimberly would take the loss. After the game, they would meet with Taro and Taylor for a few minutes. Taylor worried about Kimberly, but a quick check seemed to indicate that the young goalie was fine.

Time went by, and Portland was quiet at the trade deadline. Taylor felt that the team didn't need to make any changes, and the senior staff thought the same. Things picked up in February and March as wins kept piling up. Now, with the playoffs approaching, the team was poised to challenge for the league title once again.

Chapter 9
1998 Playoffs

Just before the playoffs started, Wayne called home. He had big news. He had been called up by Spokane, and would be riding along in the playoffs. Whether he would actually play or not remained to be seen. But, at the very least, he would gain valuable experience skating and practicing with the team. At the same time, Kimberly announced to the family that she had been called up by Seattle. Similar circumstances were at play, and she would be traveling with the team for their first round series. That meant that she would be traveling with Seattle when they faced Portland.

The playoffs started with a first round series against arch-rival Seattle. Portland started out with a bang, blowing out Seattle with a 7-3 win in Game One. Things would settle down somewhat for the next couple games, but Portland slowly wore them down, earning a five-game series victory, and, more importantly, a second round bye. This would put them directly into the Western Conference Final. While Portland waited, Spokane dispatched Prince George in four games.

On a side note, Kimberly did not suit up for Seattle in the playoffs against Portland, but she did become the first female player to be listed on a post-season roster. Another small mark in the record book for the Tsujimoto family.

The Western Conference Final would pit father against son, Portland against Spokane. Wayne had played in five of Spokane's eleven games in the playoffs to this point, and he was looking forward to facing Portland.

The series would stand tied after the first four fairly evenly played games. That was all to change in Game Five, played in Portland.

Portland would race out to a quick lead, and keep building on it. Eventually, Spokane would pull their starting goalie, but it didn't stop there. Portland would roll to a 9-2 win. It would send the fans home happy, but left just three days to prepare for the big showdown in Spokane.

Wayne scored the first goal of Game Six, and as he celebrated, he skated past the Portland bench, trash-talking and yelling at them. Taro just shook his head at what he considered poor sportsmanship.

Spokane would win Game Six, setting up a winner-take-all Game Seven.

That loss in Game Six would be the very last game Portland would lose for the rest of their post-season. Portland would hold off Spokane for a victory in Portland in Game Seven, sending the fans into absolute pandemonium.

After it was all over, and the players were congratulating each other in line, many of the Spokane players made a point of shaking Taro's hand. Many said that it was an honor to meet him. He just smiled, and walked on through the line. It was something that he was used to hearing all throughout his career. He paused for a few words with Wayne, then moved on.

Now, it was off to face the Brandon Wheat Kings for the WHL Championship.

It was almost anti-climactic by this point. Only one game was determined by less than four goals. Portland blew out Brandon 7-3 in Game One, and rolled up a similar score in Game Two. By the time the two teams reached Brandon, Manitoba, the series was half over, and Portland pretty much sealed it with a 7-2 blowout in Game Three. While Game Four was close, a one-goal affair, it was too little, too late for Brandon, who would fall in a four-game sweep.

A week later, Portland was back in Spokane for the Memorial Cup Tournament. The winners of the three Canadian Hockey Leagues, in Ontario, Quebec, and out in the Western Hockey League, would get together along with a host team. This year's host team was Spokane.

Wayne was added to the Spokane roster for the Memorial Cup Tournament, but it was unclear how much he would actually play. As it turned out, Wayne would not play for Spokane in the tournament. He was there as an injury replacement, as well as for experience in practice. Each team would play the other teams once, and the two teams with the best record would advance to the final game. If needed, a tie-breaker or semi-final would be played.

Portland would win their first game handily, while Wayne's Spokane club would win theirs as well. However, when it was all said and done, Spokane would finish the first part of the tournament with one win and two losses, while Portland won all three of their games. Still, until the semi-final, there was still a chance for Spokane. But they would lose in overtime, and Portland would meet the winner from the Ontario Hockey League, Guelph.

Taylor and all the kids were in Spokane for the tournament final. It was going to be a crazy game, with both teams keeping it fairly close down the stretch. The game would go to overtime, and Portland would ultimately come out on top.

As the winning goal was scored, the Portland side exploded as the players leaped off the bench, threw their gear in the air and raced into the corner to celebrate their victory. Taro and the rest of the coaching staff also celebrated. Taro had now won a Stanley Cup and a Memorial Cup. It was quite an achievement for his career, especially when you consider that he wasn't given any chance of making it in North American hockey in the first place.

A few days later, back in Portland, Taro introduced the team to the fans that were gathered at the Coliseum for the celebration. The Memorial Cup trophy was brought out, and a good time was had by everyone present. A number of the fans present even asked Taro for his autograph. Apparently, after all this time, he was still well-remembered, and fondly.

He would have a meeting with team management in about a week that, along with one other incident, would change the direction of his career, and his life.

Championship ring measurements were taken from all the eligible players and coaching staff just after the tournament. Taro and Taylor would both soon add a Memorial Cup Championship ring to their collection. But things were brewing behind the scenes.

A sudden resignation in the front office had opened the position of General Manager. That would be filled by none other than Taylor Tsujimoto, effective immediately. She would be the first woman in that position in league history. Some questioned whether she was ready for such a promotion, having only served one year as assistant. She maintained that at least she had an idea of who was on the team's list of players and what to look for in regards to the future. It made sense, and the announcement was set to be made the following Friday, eight days away.

That's when the depth charge dropped. She had asked Taro to take over as her assistant. She apparently sold the team on the idea, because they both appeared at the press conference. Taylor remembers:

"I know that it was a big day when the team said that they wanted to promote me. The kids were all at the press conference, dressed to the nines. I think it was the first time in months, if not a year or more, that Kimberly wore a dress. All of them sat on the side of the room, watching the proceedings, not sure what was going on, but knowing that they wanted to be there.

Finally, it came time for the announcement. First, Taro was introduced as assistant General Manager. He said a few words, then sat back down. He was never big on speeches. The simple announcement that I was taking over as GM surprised everyone. I handled a few questions, and that was that. Taro and I were now in charge of the team, making trades, signing players, basically we were going to lead the team in a new direction."

Taro remembers it from basically the same perspective:

"The idea that I could even be considered to be General Manager material at one point was, to put it mildly, insane. I always thought of myself as a player. So, I played. Then, someone thought I might be a decent coach. So, I became a coach, but an assistant coach. I guess I did all right at that as well. Now, they wanted me to become assistant General Manager of the team. It's not that I minded working with or under a woman. I've never had a problem with that. Of course, the fact that it's my wife, Taylor, who would be my ultimate supervisor, didn't change anything either.

I just simply didn't think I was ready for this sort of career change. Taylor sold me on the idea one night while we were out for dinner. Taylor would handle most of the phone calls, the discussion and generally the day-to-day business. I would go on the road and handle some scouting and recruiting. She talked me into it and sold me on the idea of taking the reins and learning from her. For the first time in our lives, she was going to lead the way in a hockey manner and show me how it all worked.

Well, that pretty well sealed the deal. If Taylor could make it work, then I sure could do it as well."

As you can see, Taro was rapidly warming to the idea of taking a behind-the-scenes handle of the team. It was going to work, he just needed to get out there and do it.

It would be the next great challenge, a challenge as great as making it to the NHL when he started his illustrious hockey career.

For the next two years, Taro learned how to be a hockey General Manager. He discovered that he had a lot of the skills already in place. He was often dispatched on the road for scouting purposes, and used his experience as a hockey player to evaluate potential trade material.

Portland would follow their championship season with a very disappointing 5th place in the division, and lost in the first round of the playoffs. No one was very happy with such an early exit, and the team promised to redouble their efforts to try and recover.

On a personal note for the family, in the summer of 1999, Taro watched as both of his younger sons, Steve and Danny, were drafted by WHL teams. Steve was taken by Seattle in the third round. He had the potential to be a teammate of his older sister, Kimberly.

Danny, however, fell a few more rounds. When the seventh round finally came around, Taro would make the announcement himself.

"With our seventh round pick, Portland selects Dan Tsujimoto."

All four of Taro's kids had now been drafted or signed by teams in the U.S. Division. Taro recalls:

"I know some people are going to say that Danny was drafted by Portland because he's my son. That has nothing to do with anything. He was available and was definitely on our list of players that we wanted to consider. He has plenty of skills and talent, and I believe that he's going to be a skilled player in the future.

I hope that all of my kids do well in the league, but I want Portland to win, first and foremost. That's never going to change as long as I am with the franchise. But it will never change the fact that I want the kids to do well. They should have every chance to succeed at whatever they choose to do, and if it's playing hockey, then I want to see them succeed. But they will have to do it on their own merits."

Things got even worse for Portland the following season,

and in 2000, the team finished with a 7th place record, last in the division. Needless to say, they did not make the playoffs. Taro was not happy about that for a moment. He vowed to double his efforts and get back to where he knew Portland should be, closer to the top of the division.

With all of his kids playing in the same division, it was a little easier to keep in contact with them, and he would have a chance to see them every time they came to town. They were all beginning to star in their own rights. Wayne was turning into a playmaker with Spokane, becoming a player much like his father. Kimberly had a slower start, but would cement her place in the record books by playing in nine regular season games, gaining five wins. She even recorded three assists and a shutout in those games. Kimberly spent the off season preparing to challenge for the starting goalie spot in Seattle the following season.

Steve was becoming a so-called "power forward." He wasn't afraid at all to blast through opponents in an effort to knock the puck loose or clear space for his teammates.

As for Danny, his first year with Portland was admittedly one to forget, only because the entire season was one to forget.

Portland bounced back the following season, and would go all the way to the League Championship Series, losing to Red Deer. Unfortunately, they would lose in five games, ending a magical ride. Still, Taro and the rest of the front office staff had good reason to be pleased.

That optimism came crashing back to earth the following season. Despite the team winning their division, the team lost in the very first round of the playoffs, leaving a very bitter taste behind as everyone headed into the summer.

This futility would be the norm for three more seasons. Out in the first round of the playoffs wasn't what Taro and Taylor had been hired to work toward.

Worse yet, with new ownership coming in, there was a lot of doubt as to whether they would even stay with the team.

Chapter 10

The 2005-06 season brought a little progress, as Portland would make it to the Western Conference semi-final before bowing out of the post-season. Unfortunately, that was the best the team would achieve for the next two years. One round, and done. Not exactly what anyone had been expecting.

Things got worse. The team was sold, and new people took over.

New ownership came in, and was very determined to cut costs and reduce staff whenever possible. Immediately after taking over, the new owners had a meeting with Taylor and Taro. Things didn't go well. Taylor remembers it vividly:

> "The incoming team President made it clear that he didn't need Taro and myself around together. I told him that we were a package deal. We had been working together for enough years that we could anticipate

almost everything the other person was going to do. That was worth more than money in our book. We even offered to take a pay cut to stay with the team. Finally, after about twenty minutes of discussion, the truth came out. They just didn't want a woman for a General Manager. But, they were willing to leave me in that position, with the understanding that Taro would be groomed to take over in the near future. Without much choice in the matter, I agreed to those conditions."

Taro remembers things in a similar fashion.

"It was a witch hunt from the very beginning. Those new guys did everything in their power to force Taylor out of her position. It didn't matter that everyone else around the team liked her and wanted her to stay. They already had it in for her. It was obvious that Taylor didn't have much more time with the team, but she somehow negotiated a three-year transition period. Basically, she talked them into giving her three years to stay on the job and prepare me to take over at that point. I thought it was a genius move. I knew that I could take over at any point, but I didn't want to stay with the team if Taylor wasn't going to work with them in some capacity. I actually began to consider looking elsewhere. The kids were off on their respective hockey careers. That meant that we would be able to pick up and move somewhere else, if we desired."

So it was clear that new management didn't like Taylor. Of course, it goes without saying that if they didn't like Taylor as a General Manager, then Taro wasn't going to be very happy either.

But things were changing quickly in Portland. In 2008, after less-than-stellar management by the aforementioned ownership group, the Western Hockey League stepped in and forced a sale of the team. The new owner was a billionaire oilman from Alberta. The new team president had experience in pro hockey, having helped guide Carolina to a Championship in 2006. So, a winning attitude was in place from the beginning. Taylor remembers a very important discussion:

"I was asked by the incoming President about my status. Not sure what they were talking about, I jokingly responded that I was married. That broke the ice. Turns out they wanted to know if I was planning to stay as GM. I indicated that I wanted to stay, but that previous management had made it clear that I was on my way out. Apparently, that was no longer valid. I was going to stay as General Manager, and Taro would remain as the Assistant General Manager. Taro would be the one going to go out on some scouting jobs, while I was to remain in town more often. That suited me just fine. I didn't like the idea of going very far from home. I was assured that I would only take short scouting trips, while Taro got the long missions. Apparently, they wanted Taro to be a "big gun" when it came to scouting missions. He was to be the big name to go out and try and convince players to sign with Portland. When the chips were on the line, Taro was the "go-to" guy. He relished the opportunity. I could see it in his eyes.

Something else was going on, something that no one other than Taro was aware of at that time. I had been diagnosed with MS, multiple sclerosis. It was in a very early stage, but it was clear that it was eventually going to affect my mobility. For now, though, it wasn't very serious. People in the office were very patient with me when I broke the news at a meeting. Everyone pledged to help me out with the mundane tasks around the office. The new team President made sure that if I needed something to help me with my work, it showed up right away. We're talking items such as voice recognition software. I know that the first day I showed up in my wheelchair, everyone was helpful and patient almost to a fault. But it was nice to have people waiting on me every so often. They really went the extra mile, and I can't thank them enough.

I can tell you one thing. It was nice to work with professionals again. That made us both feel appreciated."

Taro was of the same opinion:

"When I heard that the team had been sold, and there was new ownership coming in, I prepared myself to hear that Taylor was leaving the team. At the very least, I figured they wouldn't want anything to do with a woman in such a high-power position in this league.

Apparently, I was about as far away from the truth as I could get. They wanted both of us to stay on, in our same positions. I was going to do some of the high-profile scouting and recruiting, on the theory that a big name like me would be able to help reel in the prospects. Taylor might go on some shorter trips, although after she told them about her MS, they backed off on that statement.

I remember Taylor telling me, over dinner, that it was refreshing and pleasing to be working with true hockey professionals again. I had to agree."

It was clear from the first days that the new owners liked Taylor and Taro. The team itself didn't do very well on the ice with the new group in charge, but it would take time for a new coaching staff to find their mojo. So when the team finished last in the Western Conference, it wasn't a total shock.

Things would begin to turn around the following season, as the team made a dramatic leap in total points, going from 43 to 91, a 48 point increase and biggest single-season increase in team history. Taro's talents as a scout and recruiter were paying off dramatically. A number of lower draft picks were signing with Portland, and turned out to be amazing finds. It was obvious that Taro and Taylor had a team of scouts that were skilled at finding diamonds in the rough. It was clear that this was going to be a team to be reckoned with in the very near future.

A couple of controversial trades raised the ire of many fans, but the end result was a playoff berth. Not only that, but the team finished just six points out of first place, despite their fifth place finish. It was a very tightly contested division, for sure.

Portland even pulled off a seven-game, first-round upset

of Spokane before finally falling to Vancouver in six games in the second round. Was it the finish they wanted? No. Was it a huge improvement over the last few years? Definitely. It gave the fans, the players and staff something to look forward to as the summer approached.

During the summer of 2010, Taro and Taylor took a week-long vacation to Switzerland. Ostensibly for pleasure, they also had a chance to watch a few players in action. One player in particular would soon be drafted in the Import Draft, a process that allows each team to draft two players from overseas. It's designed to limit the number of players from outside North America, and allow the Canadians and Americans to develop further in this league.

Taro and Taylor turned on the magic, promoting Portland fiercely. They also pointed out the fact that there was already one Swiss player on the Portland roster, something which would ultimately help seal the deal.

With that successful scouting trip finished, they returned home to a team that was ready to challenge for the League Championship. Portland won their division by one point, but it wasn't evident in the playoffs. Portland would stomp their way through the entire Western Conference, ultimately making it to the League Finals.

Unfortunately, they would get stomped themselves in

five games. It was a rude awakening. On the other hand, it was a learning experience that would prove to be useful in the long run.

Chapter 11
2011-12 Season

With the new season dawning, it was time to bear down and focus on the goal; winning it all. Portland had an excellent roster of skilled players, and everyone knew their role.

While Portland would ultimately miss out on the division title by two points, it didn't matter much. Portland would blast Kelowna in a four-game sweep. The next series, against Kamloops, was much more competitive, and probably gave a lot of fans a lot of heartaches. Portland would jump out to a three-to-zero series lead, only to watch Kamloops win the next three games. This would set up a seventh-game, winner-take-all game in Portland. The Hawks would close out the series in a tightly contested two to zero game. The fans would applaud the visitors for their effort, a classy move.

This brought up the Western Conference Finals again, and, just like the previous year, Portland would win. This time, they won in a four-game sweep, sending them back to the WHL Finals, where they once again faced Edmonton. It went back and forth until the seventh game. Taro and Taylor went up north for the last game of the series. Taro remembers:

> "First, I have to say that it was a little strange being back in the city where I had starred as a player so many years ago. As for watching Portland play this time, it was a little nerve-wracking, sitting there cheering for the visiting team. But as Edmonton started to pull away late in the game, I found myself wishing for a miracle. Unfortunately, that miracle never arrived, and Portland lost. I have never felt so helpless in my life, watching my team leave the ice with their heads down. I didn't say anything to anyone on the team during the plane ride home. I didn't have to, as it was evident how everyone was feeling."

Taylor remembers pretty much the same thing:

> "It was fun to go to a road game with so much on the line. But as the game wore on, it was becoming clear that Portland wasn't going to be able to make a miracle happen. I think Taro took it harder than I did.

He had helped recruit some of these players, and he took the events of the Finals personally.

After the game, after we were home, I tried to console him. It didn't work very well at first, but he quickly came back around."

That wasn't the only thing brewing up during the summer of 2012. There was a group poking their noses around the Portland team offices, at the request of the WHL front office. While it wasn't clear what was being investigated, the team had been ordered, very simply, to comply with any and all requests made by this group.

To make matters worse, not only was that going on, but Taylor announced that she was resigning her position on July 1st. Taro had no warning of it. The first he knew was at dinner, at home, the night before. He remembers:

> "All I knew was that she had a hastily called press conference for a Friday at about 2pm. The only reason she gave for leaving was for 'medical reasons.' She announced that she was leaving me as Assistant General Manager, and was resigning immediately. I got left holding the bag, so to speak. I began to wonder what was going on. I started to ask a few questions of

our Head Coach, who was also going to be taking over as General Manager. He dodged me for almost a week before I changed my tactics. I went straight to the team President. He told me that he couldn't comment in the office and wasn't able to say anything. He then hands me a post-it note. On it, he had written, 'meet me outside by the fountains across the plaza.'

This is weird, but I went outside to talk with him. He tells me that Taylor knows what's going on, and if I don't want to get caught up in things, I should follow her lead and let it all happen away from me. No doubt, I could come up with something medical as well, or something equally plausible. Basically, he would guarantee the remainder of my contract if I left by the end of June. If I stayed past July 1st, there would be no guarantees about my longevity. I pressed for more details, but he stopped me right then and there and walked away."

Taro was suddenly worried. That evening was a very tense evening at the Tsujimoto home. With all the kids gone, Taro and Taylor were able to speak aloud. It didn't take long for Taylor to finally admit that she had some idea of what was going on. Taylor remembers things this way:

"I knew that the league was poking around the team offices for a couple weeks. That was obvious. They introduced themselves almost like the KGB, or some sort of secret police. When I pressed for details, they said that a recently-traded player had asked questions of his new team in the U.S. Division, up north, in Washington. When the team wasn't able to provide the same answers that Portland had given, the team in question went to the league office and alerted league officials to these odd answers. That apparently prompted the league to send in the "goon squad." All of a sudden, Taro nods. He gave me a name, and I knew who was, at least in part, responsible. I can't say the name because it wasn't officially announced, and the league probably wouldn't like me to announce it anyway.

I told Taro that I had heard that the league was already considering sanctions against Portland. I decided to up and leave right away. Yes, it would look weird. Yes, it was going to seem suspicious to many people, but I had to get out while I had the chance. I wanted Taro to do the same as well. I was sure that he and I would be able to find hockey positions elsewhere should we wish to pursue something like that in the

near future."

It was clear that Taylor was aware of things going on. Perhaps she cut a deal with the investigators. She's never commented on that, so all a person can do is speculate. Taro chose to take the same silent road as Taylor, and clams up every time the subject is broached. Neither of them will speak about the subject, the team won't talk about it, and neither will the league office. The entire truth may never be known unless either of them speaks about the issue. At the time of this writing, neither Taylor nor Taro had chosen to speak in any detail about it.

Ultimately, the league would rule against Portland, stating that the Winterhawks committed rules violations. They had bantam draft picks taken away for several years, and the head coach was suspended for the entire remainder of the season, plus the playoffs. Taylor and Taro both came under scrutiny from the league. However, it was ultimately determined that they were not involved in the inquiry, except as people in high ranking positions that were questioned. Taro had not promised anything to any incoming player, other than a chance to crack the roster in the fall each year to any player that he would speak with, and that helped his case. He also had paperwork for almost fifty players, each sheaf showing that the player understood nothing was guaranteed other than a place at either rookie camp or training camp, depending on the player's skill level. Taylor had not gone out on anything more than simple scouting trips, and always let Taro handle the face-to-face communications.

It was unfortunate that Taro and Taylor left the team when they did. Portland would go on a tear through the league and blow through the playoffs as well. Portland would win a third straight Western Conference title, and face Edmonton in the WHL Finals for the second straight year. This time, however, Portland would emerge the winner. It was sweet revenge for last season's loss.

This would earn them a spot in the Memorial Cup tournament. While the team would advance all the way to the championship game, their opponents, Halifax, would ultimately prevail. Still, the team was able to hold a big celebration party in the middle of town at the beginning of Rose Festival. The team, and fans would crowd Pioneer Square, in the middle of downtown Portland, and celebrate the season. Taro and Taylor would make a brief appearance at the celebration, but quickly melted into the background and disappeared into a restaurant for lunch, waiting for the crowds to dissipate.

It was somewhat disappointing to end the season on this note, but at the same time, it was the way that Taro had ended his NHL career. He had finished in Buffalo, and quietly moved away. Now, again, he was quietly slipping into the background.

Chapter 12

Taro held a family reunion of sorts during August of 2013. Three of the kids were present for the event.

Wayne was still single, although he had been in a very serious relationship for a couple years now. He was an assistant coach with the hockey team in Seattle, a rival of Taro's Portland club.

Wayne's hockey career had been filled with speed bumps. He gained a reputation for hard, sometimes dirty hits. At least, that was what the league thought. Wayne had been suspended three times for at least five games each time. On the other hand, he also had a rep for scoring important goals, the sort that make a team want to acquire you for a deep playoff run. He never suffered from a lack of contract offers, but there was always the worry that he would seriously hurt someone with his next hit.

Ironically, it was a low, dirty hit that would end up ending Wayne's playing career. In a mid-season game against Boston, Wayne was hit from behind in the corner by a rookie forward. This rookie, named Evan, drilled his knee into the back of Wayne's knee. While Evan only received a two-game suspension, Wayne's season was over at that point, and his career would eventually come to an end two seasons later when Wayne was unable to finish his comeback attempt due to several knee surguries and ongoing knee problems. While no one has conclusively been able to say for certain, there is a definite feeling that Wayne has never forgiven Evan for ending his career. The two players met at a charity hockey function in Boston not long after Wayne retired. Evan and Wayne stood nose to nose for several seconds and finally, after the face-off, Evan gave a rather rude shove to Wayne and told him to "buzz off." Wayne chided Evan, saying that he should appreciate those who played before him. Evan's response? A feeble attempt at a right cross to the temple. The two had to be pulled apart, and Evan was last seen screaming obscenities toward Wayne.

    As for the present, rumors persisted that Wayne was on a fast track to be a head coach in a few years. He was enjoying his time in Seattle as an assistant coach. He and his significant other, a real estate wizard named Bonnie, relaxed in a pair of patio chairs, at one end of the patio.

    Kimberly was single but taken, Now, having won three Southern Professional Hockey League titles in seven years, as well as Olympic Gold with the U.S. Women's hockey team, she was ready to pursue a challenge even bigger than hockey; she was starting to settle down. Kimberly had become one of the most decorated American women in ice hockey. The medals, awards and SPHL awards in the spare room at her place proved to be a testament that women could play in hockey at any level, if they were good enough. She also spent some time, in high demand, on the summer speaking circuit. She'd returned to Portland and got a job as a goalie coach with Portland's hockey team. In the summer, she also worked with a Portland-area hockey school, helping train goalies. She had just started seeing someone, the assistant manager at an ice rink across the river in Vancouver, Washington, but she was at the house solo on this day.

Steve had toiled with Florida's minor league system before being traded to Anaheim. The trade re-energized his career, and he had been playing on the second line since the trade, as well as helping train the younger players on the club for a few years since the trade. He was married to a beautiful actress named Toni, and they had three kids. Toni was four years older than Steve, and brought the kids from her first marriage. She had appeared in modest roles in about a dozen roles in various movies, and had just signed a three year deal to appear as a recurring character on a popular sci-fi television series. Steve's kids were tossing a football around Taro's rather large yard. Toni was away in Texas on location filming the series.

...and then there was Danny. Oh, how the fates turned on Danny.

A third round draft pick by Pittsburgh, and a ton of potential. But cracking the pro roster in Pittsburgh had been a problem for three years. So, he had opted to play hockey in Germany, and did well for three seasons. With a little help from Wayne and Steve, he had a gained a tryout with Dallas, and was on his way back to the United States to start working out with his brothers when disaster struck. Danny was on board a plane that disappeared over the North Atlantic. After three days of searching, wreckage of the plane was eventually spotted to the southwest of Iceland, and it was quickly learned that all aboard had perished. Taylor remembers that awful moment when she heard the news:

> "There's nothing in the world like waking up in the middle of the night to find out that one of your kids has been killed in a plane crash. I woke Taro and told him the news. He took it hard for days. I know that he threw himself into a lot of work at home for quite some time. I gave him a lot of space, and he seemed to understand.
>
> I called the rest of the kids and told them the news. Steve took it extremely hard. He and Danny had always been very close, being twins. All the kids were hit pret-

ty hard, of course. We were always a fairly close-knit family, and I guess this brought us closer yet."

Taro remembers it from his perspective:

"Taylor broke the news to me about Danny and the plane crash. She took it hard, as did all the kids. Steve, especially, was hit hard. I expected that, as it was his twin brother. They had been extremely close their entire lives. There's nothing worse for a parent than to hear that one of your kids is now dead, and there was absolutely nothing that you could have done to help."

Steve had a few words to share about his twin brother:

"I just can't explain the shock and horror of hearing about Danny's death. No parent or family member should have to hear about a loved one being involved in such an event. I followed the story closely for days, even weeks. Something had gone wrong on the plane, one of the engines completely blew apart, and it sounds like the resulting damage blew holes in the wings and caused the plane to go down.

I lost my twin brother that day. They weren't

even able to bring his body home for us to have at the service. When the wreckage slammed into the ocean, much of it was either blown apart on impact, or sank to the bottom of the ocean. Only a miniscule number of bodies were recovered. I will live with the thought that Danny's last minutes of life were probably experiencing great terror and pain before being snuffed out by the great ocean."

Postscript

It's clear that Taro and Taylor grew very close together over the years. Getting married in the summer of 1983, and growing even closer over the years is something that many couples only hope to achieve.

After more than thirty years, the pair has grand-kids already, and no doubt there are more that will arrive eventually. Hockey will probably always play a part in their lives to some degree. They still attend games in Portland every so often. Taro will still sign pucks or other items for the booster club to raffle off as prizes. Taylor is remembered as a top-notch General Manager, one who helped put together a championship-caliber team.

When the team won the League Championship, they gave out souvenir replica title rings to season ticket holders. In spite of their quick exit, the team gave real ones to Taro and Taylor, just like the team received, as a way to say thank you for everything that the couple had done.

Will Taro ever go back behind the bench, or get into the

GM office again? He maintains that he doesn't want to, but something in his eyes gleams when he turns it down. Taylor probably won't. Over the last couple years, her MS has made it difficult to be at a desk full-time. Taylor doesn't like to go out in a wheelchair often, so she stays at home a lot. One exception is hockey. She's still extremely active with the booster club and attends many of the home games during the season. Taro helps out as well. Taylor is also adamant that she won't take any GM-type of job if she can't give it 100%, and she isn't able to do that these days. Some doubt that she would ever take on such a responsibility again.

Buffalo contacted Taro and asked him to come back for one night. The Sabres wanted to retire his jersey. Initially, he didn't want to go. Taro claimed that he wasn't deserving of such a reward. Taro recalls:

> "I didn't think that I had earned that reward, to have my number retired. Sure, I was good, but so were a lot of other players in Buffalo history. I didn't feel that my abilities had made me that much better than anyone else. Once they retire your number, it hangs there forever, for everyone to see it and think about how good you were. I didn't want people debating my skills for years to come. But I finally began to realize that it was a huge honor, and I should accept it. Tay-

lor helped a little bit with my choice, sure. But to be honest, I began to like the idea of being immortalized. It was one last thing that Buffalo could do to honor me, and I was going to go ahead and accept the highest honor a team can give a player."

After much reservation, and probably more than a few words from Taylor and the kids, he relented. Taylor would join him on the trip to Buffalo to watch number 74 being raised to the rafters. It was a touching moment for the former Sabres forward. Taro remembers the magical night:

"Taylor was by my side as the lights went down and we followed the carpet to the ice. For the evening, Taylor decided to put her pride aside and use her wheelchair. It was a little strange, standing behind Taylor's chair, one hand resting on her shoulder. It wasn't the way that we had envisioned things after all this time. By that, I mean that I never, for the life of me, expected that I would have played long enough or well enough to be worthy of having my number retired. But, to be fair, time does this sort of thing to people.

We took our spot and watched a video package of my career. I was definitely moved by the highlights, remembering all the teammates I had played with over the years. Then the surprises started to appear.

Danny and Lee walked out from the other end of the ice to thunderous applause. We embraced, and smiles were shared all around. Clint walked out to a huge roar from the crowd and gave me a huge hug. I was so pleased to see him on the ice, especially since I had read about his multiple life challenges since getting his neck cut by a skate blade so many years ago. Then came the last, and biggest surprise. It was totally unexpected when the lights came up.

From my end of the ice, Steve's wife, Toni, and their kids walked out on the carpet. Steve skated up from somewhere in the darkness. I gave everyone hugs. Taylor stood up, clearly hurting from her MS symptoms and gave a hug to Steve and his family. Steve's kids looked so cute with Buffalo jerseys on for the occasion. Wayne skated out next, and we hugged him as well. But the biggest surprise was the appearance of Kimberly. The last we had heard, she wasn't going to be able to make it, as she was supposed to be coaching Portland's goalies early in the season. Not that I was going to argue. It was wonderful having almost the entire family together for one last appearance on the ice. Wayne held up a sign with Danny's name on it, plus his birth and death year, and a large RIP. This was the best we could do for our fallen son. We posed for pictures, and then I turned to face a large rectangular box sitting on the ice.

From the PA announcer, came the following:

"Now, Taro, let's raise that banner." I took the handle, as I had been coached earlier in the evening, and slowly began pulling. My name was at the top of the banner, and my number 74 was underneath, with the years I had played in Buffalo at the bottom. The fans got louder and louder the higher the banner went, and finally the banner had reached the peak of the building. There was a standing ovation for several minutes. I stood in the spotlight, unashamed to let the emotion show on my face. I turned to Taylor, still standing but hanging onto me, wrapped my arms around her and kissed her, right there in front of the entire building. As Taylor sat down in her wheelchair, I knew I had to say a few words to the fans.

'To everyone who supported me from the beginning, and throughout my career, I want to say something to everyone, one last time. 'Taro says, thanks everyone!'. Thank you for helping make a Japanese boy's dream come true.'"

The "Taro says," remark just about brought down the house. Signs were all over the place, and Taro would spend the first intermission signing jerseys, buttons, signs, almost anything the fans brought to him. It was a fitting end to his pro career.

Three weeks later, back in Portland, Taro and Taylor were honored as builders in the Portland Winterhawks Hall of Fame, for their work as general managers, plus Taro's work as an assistant coach. It was almost a repeat of the ceremony in Buffalo. Portland management really outdid themselves. Taro's family, as well as Taylor's parents, were present on the ice. A video package of the team's accomplishments while Taro was a coach with the team played. A few players that he had coached were present and skated out to greet him on the ice. Wayne and Steve appeared by video, as they were off at their respective NHL camps. The team did a wonderful pre-game presentation and unveiled a banner with his name on it. Finally, it was time for speeches. Taro guided Taylor to the podium. She stood, and holding tightly to the podium, she spoke first.

"I'm just a Canadian country girl from Edmonton. All I did was smile at a guy who looked like he needed one. We talked awhile, and I decided that I wanted to get to know him better. That little move, a little caring, and that simple action, well, it led to more than thirty years married to a great hockey player and an even better overall person. This team showed foresight and courage in naming me the first female assistant General Manager in league history. When they elevated me to General Manager, that showed even more courage. I hope that I didn't let anyone down. It's never easy to take a job like that and succeed. I think I did all right. Thanks to everyone who's helped me along the way. Thanks to my kids for showing me that you can do anything you want to do in life. Thanks to Wayne, Kimberly and Steve for being just a phone call away when I needed someone to chat with while Taro was busy. A special thanks to my dearly departed son, Danny, who showed me that life is fleeting, and that every single one of us should live life to the fullest. Remember, today is called the present, because tomorrow is never promised. To all of you out there tonight, Taylor says, 'go get 'em!'"

Taylor turned and hugged Taro tightly to the sound of nearly eleven thousand people cheering. She was now almost in tears, moved by the emotion from the fans, and the emotion in her speech as well. Taro helped Taylor back to her chair. Now, Taro had to speak. He took a deep breath and turned to the fans:

> "In 1974, a Japanese player was drafted by Buffalo. Against all odds, he made the pro ranks and succeeded in carving out a career, winning three championship trophies along the way. I even had my number retired, and was elected to the Hockey Hall of Fame. If that isn't the North American dream, I don't know what is. Fate dropped me into Portland. I took that opportunity and ran with it. It's been quite a ride. Thank you to everyone who has been part of my career. Taro says... thank you everyone."

The entire building went absolutely crazy for Taro and Taylor. Kimberly walked out on the carpet and presented both of her parents with special Hall of Fame rings. She had been chosen because she was in town, as the team's goalie coach. The other two boys were busy at their respective training camps. They all posed for pictures during thunderous applause.

It was a fitting end to Taro's hockey days.

Retirement can be a scary time, especially for a pro athlete. The unknowns of the world can make things uncertain and unclear. Will Taro or Taylor ever return behind the bench or to the front office? No one knows for sure, but it would seem unlikely at this time.

Taylor has spent a lot of time working with Portland's Booster Club. She calls it easy work helping promote raffles, giveaways, and road trips. She hasn't been on the bus trips herself, due to limited mobility, but she helps organize them. Instead, Taro and Taylor will drive on their own to a game or two. It's easier to go on their own schedule. Besides, if Taro calls ahead, the other team often rolls out the red carpet for him and Taylor.

On occasion, Taylor will help arrange for a signed Taro puck to make its way to the Booster Club. 'Taro Says...' buttons are still a fairly hot item, and signs can be seen at most home games.

Taro spends a little more time at home these days, but often he is spotted walking the concourse at home games. Sometimes fans who remember watching him play will stop and ask for an autograph or picture, and he will almost always pause for them.

So, keep an eye out when you are in Portland at a hockey game. You just might happen to walk past the greatest player "never to have played the game."

SPECIAL THANKS

What you have read is fiction. Taro Tsujimoto never existed, except as a prank played on the NHL by a General Manager who was sick and tired of the draft process back in June of 1974. May he live long and successfully in these pages.

Special mention goes to George 'Punch' Imlach, the man who started the entire caper, the Buffalo Sabres General Manager in 1974. Had it fallen on April 1st, it never would have been believable. Happening at the NHL Entry Draft in June, well, that makes it easier to believe; the fact that he pulled it off, even for just a few weeks, well, that's sheer genius.

I want to give a special shout out to the folks at Third String Goalie. This is an excellent web page which highlights the odd, wacky, and interesting in hockey. They allowed me to draw from their database and use information to help fill in the biography that you have read. Check them out at www.thirdstringgoalie.blogspot.com

Another great website for information about hockey

players is <u>Greatest Hockey Legends</u>. The database of superstars, as well as those lost in the mix, is huge. There is also a large list of hockey books. Check out their website as well at <u>www.greatest-hockeylegends.com</u>

  _____Finally, I would like to wish a special thanks to my wife, Mary Lou. Her continued support has proved to be invaluable. Thanks to my friends for their encouragement as well. To all of my "hockey friends," thanks for asking me all the time about my progress. It really helped keep me moving along when I needed it most. Just a few of my hockey friends include Shelby, Stephanie, Teri and her mom, Stuart, his wife and the rest of the booster club, "Mr. Shaggy, the best dressed guy at a Portland hockey game," and all the Portland fans who will be reading this at some point. There are so many more, I can't name all of them, but thank you.

  I also want to mention, specially, Mary Lou and her husband David, NovaLee and her husband John, Amy, and Lisa. They are the closest friends that I've got. A person can always have room for a small number of the highest quality of friend. This group of people are the best.

  My family; Dad, Cindy and Wendy. In their own, individual ways, they encourage me as well. Brandon and Tyler, my step-sons, they've helped with insights on hockey from their minds. Thanks to all of you!

The Portland Winterhawks are a major junior franchise in Portland, Oregon, playing in the Western Hockey League. They have helped over one hundred players achieve their goals of playing in the NHL. They are a high-quality franchise, with quality leaders teaching the young men that come through the arena how to become better people, better players and succeed in life. All teams mentioned as playing against Portland in this story are for real. I have, for legal purposes, omitted the team names and used only the city where they are located.

I would like to personally thank Taro and his wife Taylor, plus their children Wayne, Kimberly, Steve and Danny, for their efforts in helping round out this story. Without his on-going assistance, there could be no tale of the first Japanese player to make it to the NHL.

Taro's career extended much longer than anyone expected. This is due to his constant pursuit of excellence. His excellence has paved the way for future Japanese stars to seriously consider the North American hockey leagues as a choice when pursuing hockey careers.

About The Author

Mark Hinrich is an avid hockey fan who enjoys attending the games of his hometown WHL Portland Winterhawks, located in Portland, Oregon.

He enjoys writing, reading various authors for inspiration. Mark can also be found working with All is Pawsible Service Dog School, which operates in Portland. He is the Special Projects Coordinator. He is responsible for, among many things, organizing field trips, helping out in class and assisting in preparing for upcoming lessons in class.

He is hard at work on another novel.

Made in the USA
San Bernardino, CA
15 October 2016